DATE DUE

A Masterpiece of Revenge

A Masterpiece of Revenge

J. J. FIECHTER

ARCADE PUBLISHING • NEW YORK

FIRST NORTH AMERICAN EDITION

ISBN 1-55970-430-6
Library of Congress Catalog Card Number 98–73500
Library of Congress Cataloging-in-Publication information is available

Published in the United States by Arcade Publishing, Inc., New York
Distributed by Little, Brown and Company

10 9 8 7 6 5 4 3 2 1

PRINTED IN THE UNITED STATES OF AMERICA

To my very dear brother Georges,

and in everlasting memory of

Françoise and Gilles

"In Claude Lorrain's paintings nostalgia for the past bonds with the beckoning call of the future. . . . We are drawn toward what lies beyond the horizon, toward that source of light in the sky that becomes our life's spiritual goal."

AUTHOR'S NOTE

Though the methods and techniques of scientific analysis of artworks described in this novel are based upon the latest research, this remains a work of fiction written purely for the reader's pleasure. Any resemblance between the characters and actual persons living or dead is purely coincidental and not intended by the author.

A Masterpiece of Revenge

First Sketches

Jane leapt out of bed and strode to the far wall of her hotel room. With both hands she lifted the painting off its hook. The unsightly thing had been assaulting her delicate sensibilities from the moment she'd checked in, and when she'd opened her eyes that morning there it was again, in all its hideousness. She couldn't take it for another second.

Others might have found the work in question innocuous enough. It was a depiction of Nice's harbor, showing a few boats floating on some brackish water. To Jane, however, it was an affront. How could anyone call such a monstrosity art? Why *did* hotels always insist on putting up these wretched eyesores?

"Much better," she said out loud, leaning the painting against the wall — facing away.

Jane threw open the curtains, called room service and ordered tea, then ran a bath. She turned on the radio. Ravel's *Bolero* was playing. She smiled at a memory of the time she had danced to the piece for Peter. The look in his eyes as he watched her — mesmerized, like Herod by Salome. Peter had told her she was the most beautiful woman he had ever seen. He had also left her. That was not to be forgiven.

Switching off the radio, Jane banished dark thoughts of revenge. Here she was in the south of France, the morning sun streaming through the windows. Far, far away was the dreary English winter. Today was a glorious beginning. Today she would take full command of the heart and soul of Charles Vermeille.

The day before, just off the plane from London, she had taken a taxi straight to the hotel, without so much as glancing out the window at this Mediterranean paradise where tourists milled about, mostly Northern Europeans on the run from their native winters. She had lingered for a little while in the hotel lobby, in the hope of spotting Vermeille, if only for a moment, before locking herself away in her room. She needed to be alone, to unwind after all those weeks of hard work, and to put the final touches to her presentation.

What had brought Jane to Nice was a symposium organized by the International Center for Advanced Study in the Visual Arts. The invitation to speak had taken her a little by surprise. She was aware her article in *Conservation Studies*, "Inert-Gas Preservation Methods for Paintings," had created something of a stir in the world of art restoration, but never would she have dreamed it would mean getting invited to Nice. She was but the director of a small laboratory specializing in analysis and restoration. Attending this symposium were the world's most illustrious curators and historians — Jan Kelch from Berlin, Marcel Roethlisberger from Geneva, Christopher Baswell from Yale, and . . . Charles Vermeille of the College de France.

Charles Vermeille! She still couldn't believe it was true. His work on the French landscape painter Claude Lorrain had opened up worlds of wonder to her. Vermeille single-handedly had provided a vocabulary for understanding and appreciating Truth and Beauty. She owed him so much.

Meeting Vermeille had been in her thoughts for some time now. There was a kinship between them, and though they had never met Jane had convinced herself Vermeille would instantly recognize this. She couldn't wait for the expression of surprise in his eyes. Yes, of course he would be dazzled by her beauty — all men were. But with Vermeille there would be a deeper recognition of connectedness.

She smiled approvingly at her reflection in the mirror.

First things first. To captivate Vermeille, she needed to impress her distinguished colleagues here at the conference. Doing that while discoursing on the rather dry subject of art conservation was not going to be easy. Jane felt passion for her profession. That wasn't the problem. The problem, she felt, was that her expertise was technical, not lyrical. One had to proceed methodically.

And this symposium was hardly the sort of occasion at which you could simply stand up and tell amusing anec- dotes — not that Jane would ever in the world have consid- ered talking spontaneously. She was a perfectionist. The presentation she was to give the next day had been com- posed with meticulous care. Every word had its place.

Preparing her paper had meant professional sacrifices. It had meant turning down business and taking long absences from the lab while she searched for the slides to illustrate her points.

But it would be worth it all. At last the great day had arrived. Bring on Charles Vermeille!

It was early still. The symposium didn't begin until ten. Jane decided to forget her bath and headed to the hotel's swimming pool.

She swam a couple of lengths in the tepid water. The air was alive with the scent of flowers. How sweet life could be.

Moments later, lying on a chaise longue facing the Mediterranean, she read through the information in the packet she'd been given when she registered. Inside were her name-tag, a list of guests, and the schedule and order of presentations. There she was: "Jane Caldwell, Oxford Institute for Art Research," scheduled for 4:45 PM on the first day — tomorrow. She saw that Madeline Haussmann would be speaking before her.

That was definitely not good news. Haussmann was chief conservationist for the entire French museum system. Jane had once attended a convention at which she had spoken brilliantly about her research. Haussmann's energy and erudition were prodigious. She would be a very tough act to follow. For the first time since she'd arrived, Jane Caldwell felt nervous.

She hurried back to her room and spent the day practicing her delivery.

Early the next morning Jane entered the auditorium of the convention center, located a few minutes' walk from the hotel. It was crowded with guests and conference officials.

Her heart was pounding. He was somewhere in this chaos. She scanned the crowd.

What if he hadn't come at the last minute? No, that was quite impossible. He was one of the world's experts on French art, and one of the stars of the convention. Without Charles Vermeille in attendance the whole affair might as well have been canceled. The thought soothed her, and she listened with unfeigned interest to the opening remarks given by Mitchell Ainsworth, a pioneer of radiography at the Metropolitan Museum in New York.

Jane spotted Vermeille during lunch on the terrace. He was sitting with three other guests. She nearly made up her mind to go straight up to him and tell him how much she admired him, but restrained herself. There was no reason to rush matters. In a few hours his blue eyes could feast upon her at leisure. He would see her at the lectern, looking composed and beautiful — and he would fall beneath her sway.

When she took her place at the speakers' table minutes before her talk, however, Jane's calm began to evaporate. Madeline Haussmann, damn her, had given a tour-de-force performance, concluding her talk to thunderous applause. During the short intermission that followed, those who had come only to hear Haussmann speak had left. Jane could see empty seats. She remembered what Sarah Bernhardt was purported to say before going on stage: "Bombs, war . . . dear God, anything but stage fright!"

Jane's turn came. She approached the lectern like a Christian walking into the Colosseum. Taking a deep breath, she launched into her presentation.

She opened with a catalog of the devastating effects certain nefarious agents have on works of art: microscopic

organisms, egg-laying insects, sunlight, artificial light, vibra-
tion, pollution, candle smoke, sudden variations in temper-
ature. Using before-and-after slides of paintings — which
elicited gasps from the audience — Jane proposed that pre-
ventive conservation was most urgently called for. Museums
and collections needed to find ways of monitoring and controlling the environments in which they placed their masterpieces. Their sacred duty was to care for these
irreplaceable works of timeless beauty.

Jane warmed to her subject and her stage fright sub-
sided. She was able to make eye contact with members of
the audience. There he was, sitting in the front row.
Vermeille seemed — she could tell this instantly — both
present and absent at the same time. He was listening and
watching her, his legs crossed elegantly, but he also gave the
impression of being somewhere else.

A realization struck her: to a man preoccupied by his
own thoughts, Jane Caldwell was but another speaker on the
program, nothing more. Disillusionment struck fast and
deep. Jane needed to summon all her strength to get
through the remainder of her presentation.

The applause that followed rang hollow. How hard she
found it to acknowledge the words of praise from people who
approached her afterward. All she could feel was bitter disappointment. The one person on whom she had wanted to have
an effect had, as far as she could discern, felt nothing.

Hurrying back to the hotel, Jane shut herself in her
room. She was filled with rage and also vaguely and sadly
resigned. It had something to do with Vermeille's expression of indifference. Eyes that see everything and nothing.
It was a look she knew. Her father.

With shaking hands Jane poured herself a glass of Scotch. Thank heavens she had bought some at the duty-free shop. She took a long swallow.

Perhaps he had noticed her after all. It was possible. What had she expected? That he would jump to his feet the minute she'd finished her talk and publicly declare his love? Jane chided herself for being so naive. Nobody worth having would do that sort of thing, least of all Charles Vermeille.

Feeling more in control of her emotions — and assisted by two more glasses of Scotch — Jane dressed for dinner. The program announced there would be a guided tour of Nice's old city for all the speakers, followed by a "typical Provençal" dinner at a restaurant on the harbor. Vermeille would certainly be there. Jane had in mind a new strategy. She would ignore him, in haughtily superb fashion — a mirror of the way he had ignored her.

Vermeille was not on the guided tour (Jane might have guessed it was not the sort of thing that would appeal to him), but he did join the group at the restaurant. Jane was seated when he arrived, surrounded — as she'd planned — by a group of men vying for her attention. She knew she looked stunning in her simple white dress, draped at the shoulder with a blue clasp. Vermeille's eyes met hers and for a second their gazes locked. Then someone hailed him, and he left to sit down at a table three tables from hers.

That brief look was enough to stir her heart. All was not lost. During dinner she behaved as if he were looking at her the whole time. She offered her best profile to him; she made calculated but graceful gestures; she formed irresistible smiles; she fluttered her eyelashes; she moved her shoulders sinuously. Her rapt suitors mistook these allurements as designed exclusively for their benefit, were delighted, and fawned all the more.

Jane had decided beforehand to depart abruptly after the dessert course — like a disappearing apparition, like Cinderella at the stroke of midnight. Leave them with an appetite for more, she thought.

The next morning, Jane sat in the front row of the auditorium — in the very seat Vermeille had occupied the day before. She wanted to be as close to him as possible, close enough to weave her spell.

The title of Vermeille's paper was "The Fruits of Collaboration Between the Arts and the Sciences." Jane wondered if he spoke as beautifully as he wrote. She was sure he did. It was, after all, his mind that had first drawn her to him. From photos in magazines she'd known he was handsome. A leonine head, slightly thrown back, with a powerful neck. A gaze that looked into the distance but also seemed to go to the heart of matters. Square jaw, strong, straight nose, cleft chin. Everything about him bespoke virility and authority. Jane thought he was the very distillation of masculinity.

Vermeille's voice absorbed her from the start. It was the voice of an orator — soft, vibrant, low. While he talked, his eyes lifted toward his listeners, a quiet smile signaled the innate and impeccable self-assurance with which he performed every gesture. His figures of speech were daring but always apt.

Swept along by the voice, Jane forgot all about her emotions and strategies and simply listened to what the man had to say. Vermeille's lecture compared the working methods of the seventeenth-century French painters Nicolas Poussin and Claude Lorrain. An analysis of the original designs of two particular paintings served as his point of departure. The magic of infrared spectrometry had brought to the surface what heretofore had been hidden beneath layers of paint, affording invaluable clues as to the artists' earliest intentions.

Relying on the expert work of scientists at the Städelsche Kunst Institute in Frankfurt, which owned two of these painters' masterpieces — Lorrain's *Landscape with Noli Me Tangere* and Poussin's *Stormy Landscape with Pyramis and Thisbe* — Vermeille demonstrated the significant differences between the earliest sketches for the works and their final composition, explaining why and how the hidden stylistic elements allowed the viewer to integrate certain details in other paintings by these artists.

Jane the student of art was held in thrall. Jane the woman fumed. Not once during the course of his talk did Vermeille so much as look at her — not once did his eyes meet hers, never the slightest gesture nor the smallest sign of recognition. Not once! Summoning her concentration she tried to cast a spell over him, to force her presence upon him. This might sound silly, but Jane swore it had worked in the past. She could beam her gaze upon her prey, and he, feeling its intensity, would look around in an effort to locate the source. Not this time.

After Vermeille's talk, Jane dragged herself back to the hotel, feeling as she used to when she was a little girl and her father had humiliated her for some shortcoming. Why did everything always have to refer back to her loveless childhood? Spotting her in the lobby, the organizer of the symposium approached her, an exaggerated smile on his face.

"Ah, Miss Caldwell! I do hope you will honor us with your presence at the gala dinner tomorrow evening. I have put you at the same table as Jan Kelch and Charles Vermeille."

Hope was reborn. Fate was offering a second chance. She told the man that naturally she would be attending.

All that afternoon and the following day, Jane followed the proceedings of the symposium without trying again to attract Vermeille's attention. She was conserving her energies. She needed to transform herself from art restorer into living masterpiece.

That evening, she strode into the dining room — arriving late, purposefully — resplendent in a turquoise lamé gown, her auburn hair cascading over her shoulders. All eyes went straight to her.

Vermeille's, too. He rose as Jane approached the table, took the hand she had extended to him, and gallantly helped her into the seat on his left, meanwhile complimenting her on her brilliant presentation that first day. He filled her wine glass, informing her with a disarming smile that it was a Puligny-Montrachet 1987 — an elegant and fruity wine, he pronounced. Then, evidently feeling as if he had fulfilled his host's duties, he picked up where he had left off in his conversation with the others at the table.

The dinner was a master class led by Vermeille. His subject was the frescoes in the main hall of Pamphili Palace. Vermeille expounded; everyone else listened.

"Fascinating, is it not, the role Alexander VII played in

the creation of these frescoes? How Pierre de Corntone thought up the idea of dividing the space into seven compartments in order to paint it? Why under Napoléon III the room was subdivided into three parts? How the so-called improvements have really disfigured the artists' original intentions?"

And so it went.

Forgotten, Jane listened, her soul shrinking, unable either to interrupt the flow or join in. She knew nothing about the subject and was mortified she might embarrass herself. Vermeille's other listeners behaved like the pretentious cretins they were, hanging on every word he uttered, assiduously keeping this interminable discussion alive with their spirited, unctuous questions.

So she ate and she drank. The food was exquisite. *Chartreuse de ratatouille sauce vierge et ses croûtons à la tapenade, Petits farcis au fromage blanc,* and *Blanc de moruette fraîche aux olives et à la ciboulette.* One sumptuous dish followed another, and all the while Vermeille talked on and on, never pausing in his discourse while refilling Jane's various wine glasses, which, in her misery, she drained unthinkingly. Down they went. Puligny, Corton, Chablis.

More accustomed to stronger spirits than to wine, the young woman's head began to spin well before the arrival of the dessert. She became vaguely aware that Vermeille was getting her drunk. And drunk she soon was.

She decided to pounce. Suddenly, desperately, she interrupted Vermeille and started telling him everything: how much she admired his work, and how she couldn't believe the absolute consensus of their ideas on Lorrain — wasn't it miraculous? — and how wonderfully generous, yes, wonderfully, he was in sharing a vision inspired by the master's works. And here they were at the same table. Wonderful. It was all too wonderful.

Everything came tumbling out. Jane knew vaguely that she was speaking too loudly and slurring her words, that her mascara was running, and that her hair was, as the French put it, *en bataille*.

Trying to push the hair out of her eyes, her hand caught on one of her earrings, which popped off and tumbled to the floor. This caused her consternation. She had never liked her ears; the lobes were too long, she felt. They were the one thing about her appearance she deemed a flaw. She had always kept them hidden with jewelry.

Vermeille bent down and retrieved the earring, which Jane put back on, blushing deeply, still unable to stop talking. The dam had burst.

Though her mind was swimming, Jane could see that she had awakened no signs of desire in Vermeille. His blue eyes were fixed upon her, glinting with irony and condescension. He listened with a bemused smile.

She was crushed. Pretending she was suddenly suffering from a pounding headache, she hurried back to her room before the coffee arrived.

Throwing herself onto the bed, Jane gave in to heaving sobs of rage and shame. To have met the man she most admired in the world, only to have the whole thing devolve into farce. He had gotten her drunk. And he had known exactly what he was doing. The bastard!

Jane cried herself to sleep.

* * *

Early the following morning she packed her bags. She called the organizer of the symposium to tell him that she had received an urgent summons from the clinic where her father was a patient; she needed to hurry home. How very sorry she was she would be unable to attend the closing ceremonies. By late morning she was on a plane for London.

Seeing Vermeille again would have been too much to bear. Physical revulsion brought on by a screeching hangover mingled with implacable bitterness. He had shattered her dreams, dashed any hopes that he would fill the void in her life — fill the place left by her father, her adored father, her hated father, who now inhabited a world of his own, beyond her touch.

Part I

Charles

1

Looking back now on that September morning, it is clear to me I should have heeded the omens. But you must understand, I was not one of those people who lived life bracing for disaster, straining to read dire warnings and grim portents in ordinary things. I am not a superstitious man. Walking under ladders never fazed me. If the wind blew I didn't automatically assume some storm was rising. In short, Cassandra was not a prophetess to whom I paid particular homage.

Perhaps I should have.

Anyway, the first sign came while I was heading into my kitchen to make morning coffee. A painting — it happened to be a portrait of a man by Guillaumin hanging in my hallway — had fallen off the wall. How very, very odd, I thought. Some credulous creatures might have leapt to the conclusion that this signified something ominous. Not me. I was merely irritated, nothing more.

While setting up the pieces on the chessboard — on

which, every morning, I tinker with the Tartakover Strategy — I noticed that one of the pieces was missing. A bishop. A thorough search turned it up. It had somehow fallen from its perch and rolled under the table. Again, some credulous people might ascribe deep significance to this. To the superstitious, the bishop represents dark, deep forces: a master over pawns but himself a pawn of greater powers.

Again, however, all I felt was irritation. Someone had been careless and I hated carelessness. I also hated anything, any little anomaly, that disrupted my routine.

I am not alone in loving routine. Richard Wagner used to fondle the folds of a velvet curtain every morning before setting to work. Agatha Christie devised her plots in the morning bath. Georges Simenon systematically chewed pencils, beginning at one end and working down to the other. Rossini did housework the minute he got up in the morning. If the house wasn't orderly, the mind wouldn't be either.

Every morning, like Rossini, I do a few simple chores. Then I toy with the chessboard while listening to a Haydn quartet (normally one of the three opus 77 pieces, the composer's poignantly lighthearted farewell to music). And I always drink two cups of arabica, black and very strong.

Such were the elements of my routine. Done in proper sequence, they set the day into motion.

That morning in September I was, generally speaking, in excellent spirits. I had returned from my summer vacation a few days earlier and was glad to be home. Fall was arriving, and I had always liked the season, relishing summer's poignant descent. Keats's "season of mists" was arriving. I was born in September, and it has always felt like a time of

20

fresh starts and expanding possibilities. The first whiff of crisp air gives wings to my ambitions and fills my head with fantasies. My students at the College de France, most of whom view me as little more than an illustrious but crusty old pedant, would never guess at the boyish thoughts leaping within.

Anyway, as I've said, I had just returned from vacation. I was looking forward to an existence ordered by schedules. Channeling energies redoubled their strength, I always said.

Mine was a good life. Financially, I was in very good shape. Never mind that recent fluctuations in the stock market had nibbled a little at my financial portfolio. My apartment had been repainted during my absence and was cheerful and bright. The results of the medical checkup I'd had before leaving on vacation would have pleased a man of thirty. Fit as the proverbial fiddle. I could still tuck into foie gras without a second's hesitation.

I kept myself in shape by refusing to take the elevator in my Paris apartment building, though I live on the fourth floor. Each morning, following my chess and coffee, I walk down to the ground floor to pick up my mail. This, too, is part of my routine. Quite often I chat for a moment or two with Madame Fernandez, the concierge, then climb the stairs back to my apartment.

That particular morning I was a little behind schedule. I was, so to speak, dragging my feet. Possibly because I expected two unpleasant pieces of mail: my tax assessment and the dentist's bill. No sense in hurrying to deal with disagreeable little matters, thought I. Sure enough, when I went to retrieve my mail, the bill and the assessment were both there. Ah, well, I reflected philosophically, life could be worse. Besides, there also were two postcards to distract me. And a plain white envelope with my name and address printed on a label — by a computer, from the look of it.

The first postcard showed a plate overflowing with seafood, and was signed by my friend Georges. "Enjoying myself immensely!" ("immensely" underlined three times) was the exuberant message. The other postcard showed the beach at Biarritz, packed with people. "One person in this crowd misses you," read the line from my old friend Sylvie. How sweet.

As for the plain envelope, it contained, I discovered, a photograph — a color photograph, and not a very good one, of my son, Jean-Louis, who had left some weeks earlier to begin studying for his business degree at Berkeley. Perhaps it had been taken in California. He appeared to be surfing. There was no accompanying letter, nothing on the back of the photograph, no return address. Why would anyone send me a photo of my son? The postmark indicated it had been mailed from Geneva.

A gag, obviously, though I couldn't think of anyone in Geneva who knew me well enough to play a joke on me, other than a childhood friend I hadn't heard from in years. From what I remembered, he wasn't the joking type.

I looked at the photo again to see if the young man on the surfboard truly was my son. It had been taken from some distance away — probably with a telephoto lens. Perhaps, I thought, I'm mistaken. Perhaps this is a look-alike, and someone, struck by the marked resemblance to Jean-Louis, decided to send it to me. Logical enough. But why then would they type my name on a label?

As I climbed the stairs back up to my apartment, I considered the possibilities. There had to be a simple answer. My son had given the picture to someone to mail to me, and this person had simply forgotten to add a note of explanation. Again, though, that didn't explain the label. That label made no sense. There were, of course, lots of people who had forgotten how to write by hand because of the computer, but still.

I had another thought. It was conceivable the photo had been sent to me by a girl. One of Jean-Louis's innumerable conquests, abandoned when he moved on to the next one. Perhaps she was trying to get back at him. Who knows what sort of things girls today dream up?

This hypothesis intrigued me: getting at the son by going for the father. It would mean that other photographs would follow this one, further and perhaps more intimate proof of her relationship with Jean-Louis — and her control over us both. Eventually there would be some sort of message. The poor creature was too shy to reveal herself for the moment.

Whatever the case, the photo of Jean-Louis showed him looking healthy and vibrant. I paused on the landing and stared at the handsome face of my son. Soon I was lost in pleasant memories.

I was remembering the first vacation Jean-Louis and I had taken together. His mother died of cancer when he was three, and when August came and all good French citizens leave for a month's vacation, he and I went to my sister Caroline's summer house in Auvergne. This was extremely convenient for me. What would I have done with a little boy all by myself? With its volcanic peaks and medieval forests, Auvergne is a spectacular part of France.

When Jean-Louis turned twelve, things changed. The minute we got in the car that August, to drive as usual to Auvergne, he turned to me.

"Please, papa, I don't want to go to Aunt Caroline's. I want to go surfing!"

Surfing? Good heavens. I looked at him. He was giving me one of his irresistible smiles, his eyes filled with longing and with hope. I knew this look, and it nearly always worked. There was very little I wouldn't do to make the boy happy.

There was more to it than guilt. At some point I had begun to realize that his smiles were as precious to me as life itself. His laughter was music to me. I sometimes went to ludicrous extremes to please him — games, amusement parks, treasure hunts. I spoiled him.

Surfing it would be, then. Without a word, I got on the highway and headed south. The little bully knew exactly what I was doing and was all over me, squealing in delight. I cannot remember when I felt happier than at that moment. For the first time it would be just the two of us, father and son, on the road.

By nightfall we had made it to the Mediterranean coast. We looked for a hotel where they served mussels, which we both adored, and direct access to the beach from our rooms. We found the little town of Biscarosse. I can still remember the churr of cicadas and the aroma of pines warmed by the sun.

The next morning I sent a telegram to my sister, to tell her where we were. "We've gone surfing," I wrote, practically giggling with delight at the thought of her reaction.

How wrongheaded and irritating were those friends who with good intentions offered bad advice. They told me to send Jean-Louis to summer camp so that I could go off by myself and get some rest. Many were concerned I needed to meet a woman. "You ought to be having fun," they said.

What imbeciles. They had no idea that my son was the source of my greatest happiness, and that watching him live, grow, eat, run — these were my raisons d'être. All those hours spent standing up in the surf, my shoulders getting burned by the sun, watching with pride and anguish while a small silhouette squared itself on a surfboard to do battle with the waves. Those plates of seafood we shared every evening. I remember thinking there would be only four or five summer vacations when the two of us would be together. Then would come that moment when he would announce he wanted to spend his vacation camping with friends.

We spent every vacation in each other's company — on the backs of camels traveling the Silk Road, diving into the blue waters of the Pintade, drinking coconut milk on the Marquesas Islands. We saw the Promised Land, crystal-blue desert skies, palaces painted by Carpaccio. We drank the wines of Cyprus.

And every summer I took him surfing. Jean-Louis had talent; there were competitions in Hawaii and Réunion Island. My vacations were scheduled around them. We were always together. And never, never, did Jean-Louis ask if he could go camping with friends.

Standing there on the landing, holding that photo, I felt a deep sadness. There he was, surfing, and I wasn't there with him. Someone else's camera had taken the picture. Perhaps that was what hurt the most. It was as if the photo was telling me that my days with him were over, that my son was riding the waves on his own. He no longer needed me to watch over him. Now he preferred going to Pizza Hut with his pals to sharing seafood on the shore with his old man.

"Everything comes to an end, happiness included." That was the cruel message the photo was delivering.

I believe that the reason I called Jean-Louis later that day was not worry, but jealousy. I asked him, as casually as I could, who might have sent me the picture. He told me he had no idea.

"It must be a joke, Dad."

I placed the photo on the mantelpiece and thought no more about it. After preparing my Thursday lecture, I went, as always, to the Guy Savoy Restaurant. The Guy Savoy was one of my bachelor hangouts. Every Wednesday evening I dined there in the company of my good friend Luciano. The Savoy has a wonderful ragout of mushrooms, and foie gras steeped in a truffle sauce.

That evening I planned to suggest to Luciano that we play a game of chess. A game I was determined to win. Luciano had defeated me the last time we'd played. "Defeated me" is putting it mildly; he had crushed me, rather, on the twenty-seventh move, right after I had moved my pawn to C2. All I needed was to move it to C1 to get queened, but, blinded by that ambition, I fell into his trap.

Playing with Luciano was an intellectual experience. One could never predict when and where he would set his trap. The precision and rapidity of his calculations were confounding. He planned eight moves in advance. To him chess was more than a pastime. Though Luciano was a successful corporate lawyer, his life revolved around moving pieces on a chessboard, while I played purely for pleasure, and because playing well means using your imagination and your instinct. Chess is a perfect vehicle for revenge — of the slow, quiet sort. That night I checkmated Luciano with my bishop.

A dinner at the Savoy followed by chess: here was a marriage of the pleasures of palate and mind.

A week passed. I got a long, chatty letter from Jean-Louis. He loved Berkeley, he wrote, and was being challenged by his courses. He was playing tennis again. His backhand was improving. All this pleased me. Anyone working on his backhand wasn't likely to spend evenings doing drugs at a rave in San Francisco. The more sports my son did, the more contented I was.

My mind was at rest and my work proceeded peacefully. I was planning a few trips: a short visit to the Stuker Gallery in Bern, which was seeking my counsel, followed by a day at Christie's in Dusseldorf. A private collector in London wanted me to have a look at a Poussin he'd bought. I worked on the proofs of my latest book, and was polishing an article for an art journal.

I also needed to finish my biographical entry for *Who's Who*. Generally I dismissed any suggestion of including my name in these sorts of publications. But *Who's Who* would be practical from a professional point of view, particularly to promote my credentials abroad. I didn't mind the world knowing I considered myself — and was considered — the greatest authority on the work of the French landscape painter Claude Gellée, also known as "le Lorrain" or Claude Lorrain, born in 1600 and died on November 23, 1682. I was an expert in seventeenth-century French painting in general, but the paintings of Lorrain had been my passion for many, many years.

I felt territorial about Lorrain. The artist himself had been mortally afraid of imitators, who were legion in his day, and had drawn shaded outlines of each of his paintings. He called this private register the *Libro di Veritá*, the "Book of Truth." What I was putting down about myself in the *Who's Who* entry was nothing more than the truth, the shaded outlines of my career.

Right after I'd finished I went down to get my mail. A vague feeling of unease spread through me when I retrieved an envelope that looked suspiciously like the one that had contained the photo of Jean-Louis. The label was identical. The enveloped was postmarked Rome.

I opened it. Inside was another photo of Jean-Louis, playing tennis. It had obviously been taken at Berkeley. Again, no identification, no note, nothing. Just the photo.

This nonsense was starting to irritate me. It was a tasteless joke. Or was it a joke? I shuddered involuntarily, as if a small electrical current had passed through me.

What worried me was the postmark. First Geneva, now Rome. What linked them? What did it mean? I knew at least that my theory about the absentminded friend was untenable.

Again I thought it might be from one of Jean-Louis's jilted girlfriends. Perhaps she was trying to show me that my supposedly studious son was spending all his time having fun. "See?" it seemed to be saying. "He's nothing but a playboy."

Perhaps it was from some guy who was attracted to Jean-

Louis and expressing his feelings voyeuristically, by sending me photographs.

I didn't think my son kept things from me, but what parent knows all there is to know? He didn't tell me everything that was going on in his life. Maybe he led a secret life. Did he have enemies? My mind started turning over scenarios, each more dreadful and absurd than the one before.

Whatever the case, I knew that I would receive a third photograph, and perhaps a fourth, and a fifth. Whoever was trying to get my attention had gotten it.

I determined to put an end to this by phoning Jean-Louis. I dialed the number. He answered on the eighth ring, by which point my nerves were completely on edge.

"Hi, Dad!" His voice was balm to my soul. "Sorry it took me so long to answer. I was in the shower. Just played two hours of tennis."

And there I had been imagining the worst sort of catastrophes. All because he was taking a shower.

I asked him when he had started playing tennis again. About three weeks ago, he told me. That meant the photo had been taken recently. I had intended to tell him about the new picture but changed my mind. This time it would worry him. And for no reason, very likely.

After asking him some silly questions, designed purely to gauge what I could from the tone of his voice, or to glean some detail — something that might hint at trouble or the outline of a problem — I said good-bye and hung up, feeling calmer.

The reassurance was temporary. This business of the photos had put me in a foul mood. I found it difficult to concentrate on "European Estheticism Toward the End of the Seventeenth Century," the title of my next lecture. The situation was upsetting the smooth operation of my routines, leaving me feeling disorganized and edgy.

When I least expected them, dark thoughts would swirl in my mind, a noisy chaos of them. I don't think now that I felt any specific fears of immediate danger. That was the problem. I couldn't make the photographs fit into a frame; hence there was no way of figuring out the motives behind them.

The following day I had lunch with Luciano at the Savoy. We played chess and I lost. I unnecessarily and stupidly sacrificed my bishop for a knight. I never would have done that had I not been distracted.

The third photograph arrived a week later. I opened the envelope, my heart beating hard, my ears buzzing. Only later did I note the postmark indicating it had been mailed from Brussels.

The photo showed Jean-Louis reading on a balcony, presumably that of his Berkeley apartment. It had been taken from a distance, again with a telephoto lens. My son seemed unaware his picture was being taken.

I sat down and tried to think. I couldn't even play my Haydn. Noise of any sort was disruptive. Clouds were darkening over me. A current of dread ran in my veins.

I struggled nonetheless to remain composed, for I knew that I needed to find some kind of design. I put a stray pencil back into its tray, refiled a folder lying on the desk, and plucked dead leaves off a geranium. Then I began examining the third photograph.

Instinctively, I sniffed it, hoping for the trace of an odor: a woman's perfume, or tobacco, or a chemical, something that might set me on the right track, like a bloodhound given a scent and then taken off the leash.

I examined the photograph minutely, looking for a fingerprint, a lipstick trace, a smudge of nail polish, some varnish, a stain.

I lit a match and heated the back of the image to see if something might have been scrawled in invisible ink, or if it bore the impression of some writing. Please, I begged, give me a code. Anything.

Finally in desperation I lined up the three photos and tried to make some sense of them as a series. Perhaps I needed to find the right way of reading them, of finding their meaning in their order, as if each were parts of a single sentence, visual words.

Jean-Louis surfing . . . ocean, tide, wave, undertow, drown.

Jean-Louis playing tennis . . . court, serve, double fault, overhead, put away.

Jean-Louis reading on his balcony . . . height, vertigo, fall.

When you play this kind of game, danger lurks everywhere, even in the happiest of photos. Behind the tanned skier is the tree that can kill him. Beneath the foot of the young man hugging his girlfriend is the step waiting to give way. It was silly, regressive. Still . . .

In the corner of the beach in the first photo was a brown-haired woman. Was she meaningful? Was her look malevolent?

What about the flower bushes to the left of the tennis

court in the second photo? Could they mean something malevolent, as they did in the tarot cards my grandmother used to read the future? One card had a bouquet of flowers in the corner, signifying, she told me solemnly, "Ill luck to the man who strays from the straight path." The simplest bouquet of flowers can foretell doom.

My grandmother had attempted to initiate me in the obscure arts of divination. I used to laugh, though now I think it had some influence on my choice of careers. My life revolved around the search for hidden meanings.

Symbols and signs are inscribed even in those paintings whose meanings seem self-evident. From the works of Cranach, Bellini, Piranesi, I had learned a thing or two about puzzles. I'm not talking about hidden figures, magic squares, crosses, skulls, or scales, all of which you can decipher with the help of a half-decent reference book. I'm talking about symbols that on first view don't seem like symbols at all: a color, a chubby baby, a stone terrace, a bouquet of flowers.

The *Allegory of Purgatory,* which for many years was attributed to Giorgione, then to Bellini, is a veritable hotbed of clues that yield unending interpretative possibilities. Thousands of feverish imaginations have focused on the painting, trying to account for all the arcane references and multiple meanings. To say the painting deconstructs itself is too easy an excuse for giving up.

Observing Piranesi's *Prison* or De Chirico's abandoned cities, those factories of the uncanny, we learn that the only way they can be approached is through metaphor, in an association of ideas. You find the first word, which in turn gives you the second, and so on. By a sequence of decoding, the visual turns linguistic.

Even were my son not involved, I would have spent the day poring over the photographs. I do not like being kept in the dark. Having devoted my life to deciphering the seemingly indecipherable, I know that it is possible to find meaning. The problem this time was that my judgment was clouded. Behind these photos lurked some danger. Instinct was telling me to beware.

"Premonitions are like instinct," my wife used to say. "They are infallible."

Sophie's intuitions had been infallible. She could tell if Jean-Louis was ill before the symptoms appeared. She sensed when he had a fever. She would run to Jean-Louis's crib even before he awoke in tears from a bad dream.

Thinking of Sophie made me think I should ask for advice from someone, but I did not feel I had anyone to whom I could turn. I had always been a bit of a loner. It's not that I'm misanthropic, for I'm not. I enjoy the company of good friends like Luciano and Sylvie.

But I relished solitude more. That is perhaps why I chose the line of work I did. I enjoyed being alone with a work of art, alone with its beauty — even if the work contained some wisdom I might share with my fellow man, its pleasure for me lay in the poetry of contemplation. In solitary communion with beauty one achieves the highest state of awareness.

The truth was I did not feel I could confide in anyone. Yes, there was my sister, and Sylvie, and Luciano, all of whom were above suspicion in that matter of these photographs. But I mistrusted the rest of the world. How can I confess to this? For a split second I even imagined my son was sending me these photos, as a ruse for extorting money.

That thought proved I was losing my sanity. At that instant I decided to go to Berkeley as soon as possible — the next day — and visit Jean-Louis. I had planned to return to San Francisco at some point anyway; I had an open invitation from the Young Museum to authenticate a work attributed to Le Nain.

I have said I was not a superstitious man. I was changing. That morning, on the way to the post office to mail in my article (entitled "The Play of Contrasts in Lorrain's Landscapes"), a large cat with orange fur, a magnificent creature, stopped in front of me and stared unblinkingly with its phosphorescent green eyes. I couldn't rid my mind of the image of those eyes the entire day.

I must have looked the way I felt, for the secretary and the security guard at the College both inquired after my health. I told them I was feeling fine, thank you, though the truth was that I had had to stop twice on the way to the office because my heart was beating so hard and my head felt coated in ice. I had gone into a café and ordered sugared tea. Next to me two men were talking.

One said to the other, "Anyway, I expected it. I had lived with the fear of it for so long I couldn't breathe. Everything scared me. I knew I needed to prepare for the worst. But, you know, I just couldn't face it. Every time I tried, I closed my eyes."

"There's your mistake," the other replied. "If they're threatening you, it's because they're the ones who feel threatened. Don't you see? *They're* afraid of *you*."

I swallowed my tea and stopped in at the first travel agency I could find to buy my ticket.

"I'm very sorry," an officious young girl behind a desk

told me, "but the next two Air France flights to San Francisco are fully booked."

"These planes are never fully booked. Look again, please, miss. There must be a free seat somewhere. In the middle, toward the back, I don't care —"

"Sir, I'm telling you. They're full. Not one seat is open."

I left the travel agency feeling that the world was in league against me. I decided to take matters into my own hands. Early the next morning I packed and went to the airport, where I bought a standby ticket for the first flight to San Francisco.

2

Of course there were empty seats on the first flight. There always are, especially in first class.

Getting on the flight settled my nerves a bit. I had lots of legroom, and was comforted by the idea that I would be with Jean-Louis in a dozen hours. I had called from the airport to tell him I was coming. He told me he would come meet me.

The champagne was chilled, the flight attendants cordial. I dove into an article on seventeenth-century drawings and for a while lost track of time.

Then two Americans sitting in the row behind me began talking about recent earthquakes in the San Francisco area.

This brought back all my fear. I regretted that Jean-Louis had ever had the idea of getting his business degree at Berkeley. What was wrong with the University of Michigan, or Yale? Why did he have to choose a school located, as the whole world is well aware, equidistant between the San Andreas and Hayward Faults? I knew that only one quake in ten thousand was dangerous, and that there was a million times smaller chance of being killed in an earthquake than of winning the lottery. Reminding myself of this did little good.

I recalled one California guidebook cheerfully informing me that California was particularly susceptible to earthquakes in the autumn. Here it was, the beginning of autumn. How delightful.

Where my son was involved I had always imagined the worst. I would never forget the day when he said the words that caused my heart to fall into my shoes: "Dad, I want a motorcycle."

Five little words, yet they had thrown me into total panic. Images instantly crowded my teeming brain — Jean-Louis in a coma, on a hospital bed, bleeding profusely in some gutter, broken in a thousand places. It had seemed like only yesterday he had cut himself above the eye falling off his tricycle.

And now he wanted a motorcycle! Good God. Those metal death traps that made that infernal racket. Never!

"No, Jean-Louis. Never." I had said this as calmly as I could.

"But, Dad —"

"No."

"But, *Daddy*." He began his sweet-talking routine, and I'd had to shut my ears.

Eventually, of course, I relented. I allowed myself to be dragged down to the nearest motorcycle dealer, where Jean-Louis pointed out the one he had his heart set on. It was shiny and red. The color of blood.

I had never seen such a monstrous machine, and

searched the salesman's eyes for some shred of sympathy. Nothing but the sale was on his mind. In desperation I had asked Jean-Louis if he didn't want a VCR instead, an electric organ, a drum set (to hell with the neighbors!) What about a trip to Canada? Iroquois still live in its primeval woods, you know!

All to no effect. He walked around the thing, stroking its smooth metal flanks. It was already his. That murderous salesman, who was his accomplice, sidled up to me.

"All boys want motorcycles. It's natural," he said.

The imbecile!

"All students want to study in California," Jean-Louis's professors had said years later. "It's natural."

And so off to California he had gone, putting seven thousand miles between us, a plane trip of over eleven hours. Here was the separation I had always expected and dreaded. Here was the reality: that I would wake up old, helpless, alone. I would become a pathetic old man, leading a joyless existence between phone calls from my son.

It has only been six weeks since he left, but I felt I'd already begun the long, slow journey toward death. A chill engulfed me. No more vacations together. No more evenings when I would come home with a surprise for him — a video game, a CD, an art book, fresh foie gras.

All the fun had gone out of my life. Now I was going to live with ceaseless worry and a thousand new things to fret about: earthquakes, mud slides, AIDS, drugs, religious cults, random violence. Worst was the distinct and very alarming possibility Jean-Louis would fall in love with some silly American girl and settle down with her in her native state — Arkansas, or Nevada.

In my calmer moments I understood perfectly Jean-Louis's decision to study in California. He had always dreamed of living near golden beaches, pounding surf, sequoias, the land of Jack London and the Sierra Nevada. He was happy; so should I have been. Instead of bemoaning my loneliness I should have been celebrating his happiness. Berkeley was a world-class institution. I myself had taught there for a semester before Jean-Louis's birth and I remembered well the sights and smells of California — the food and wines; the snowy tops of the Panamints; Zabriski Point, an infinite landscape whose desolation yields unexpected splendors; Badwater, near whose heated earth you could almost fry an egg; the wild roses of the Mojave.

Yes, I had sung the praises of California to Jean-Louis. I also knew that with an American business degree in hand, and then returning to France's Ecole Nationale d'administration — breeding ground of the country's leaders — Jean-Louis's future was a bright one indeed.

Of course I'd relented. It was only to be for two years. I would count the days until his return, just as I was counting the hours until the plane touched down at San Francisco airport.

Following a stopover in Chicago to refuel, my excitement began to mount. In one hundred forty-two minutes I would see him. Already I felt his proximity to me, an encroaching feeling of happiness, a wave of warmth. How fragile and tender a thing is happiness. As light as the air beneath the engines of flight.

We got a new pilot in Chicago, an American. Alas, he was a chatty fellow who felt obliged to give us a running and very homespun commentary on every aspect of the flight. Each time the public address system came on I winced.

"Captain Jerry Carter here. Well, folks, we'll be cruising at an altitude of thirty thousand feet . . . heading right smack over Kansas City. We've got real clear skies today. If you look way over on the left side of the aircraft in 'bout half an hour you'll be able to take a gander at the Grand Canyon. That's quite some sight, believe you me." I felt as if I was stuck on a guided tour.

Eventually, thankfully, the plane landed in San Francisco, and with such deft lightness that I forgave the pilot all his chatter. I headed into the terminal with a radiant smile.

There he was, just on the other side of customs, waving his arms, looking the way he used to when I came home from a trip. I was the most adored father in the world.

In the time it took to get through customs, I already knew almost everything: Jean-Louis looked happy; he glowed with good health; he was tanned and fit. When I got to him I smothered him in an embrace.

We drove into the city, talking freely and merrily. How far away my troubles in Paris seemed!

We went straight to Berkeley and to Chez Panisse. I had promised Jean-Louis in a letter that one day we would visit this mecca of California cuisine. Not only had he made the reservation, he had booked the best table, on the first floor, near the fireplace. There were fresh flowers on the table.

Time felt suspended in its flight, and I savored the delights of the moment. Warm oysters served with endive from Chino Ranch — a strange and delicious combination

Jean-Louis recommended. The boy had exquisite taste. I had made him a gourmet in my own image, weaning him on the finest and rarest of foods. Perhaps this was my way of compensating for the loss of his mother. I felt a deep obligation to teach him the art of living, and acuity of the senses, I believed firmly, was one of life's essential arts.

We sipped a fine Pinot Noir from Napa Valley, and remarked how far California wines had truly come. Nothing could compete with Bordeaux, but I knew my chauvinism was tied to a memory of a trip Jean-Louis and I had made to that region. Pine, sand, the smell of grapes, fresh foie gras. Who could forget Bayonne, with its chive purée, its black bread, its beautiful cathedral, the Bonnat Museum, and those omelets. Royan, with its oysters, its butter, and its Pineau de Charentes. Mauléon, with its wood pigeons. All this did credit to Chez Panisse, which brought back other tastes and smells.

For an hour or two I was on a cloud. Jet lag, no doubt. When dessert arrived — croissant pudding, how creative these Californians! — I began to remember why I had come.

I began asking Jean-Louis some questions I'd been rehearsing, though without trying to give him the impression that his replies were of any great moment. Who was he seeing? What did he do in the evenings? Did he go out often? Who were his friends? Simple questions. The difficulty lay in interpreting his answers. One reply can mask another.

Then I started asking questions that were less general, more probing. "Which professor do you most admire?" "Have you met someone here you genuinely dislike?"

I also asked him — in an offhand manner — if any of his

friends were addicted to drugs, or if they even took drugs recreationally. Or whether he had tried any. He answered in the negative, though a little quizzically.

"Dad, don't you trust me?"

"Of course, of course. What is there about life in America that you least like?"

I knew that my questions must have seemed a little out of character. But I felt sure that his replies would provide me with some information, a clue perhaps, anything to give me a context for those photos.

All I learned was what I'd already known — that my son was a careful young man who measured the risks before running headlong into some action. And he was no Lothario. Yes, he broke hearts, but he never broke promises. In that way, we were alike, and the realization did not hurt my vanity.

We said good night in the lobby of the Durant Hotel, a comfortable place located near the university.

"You know, Dad," Jean-Louis teased, "there have been at least fifteen small earthquakes since your arrival. Have you at least stopped worrying about that?"

I burst out laughing. It was true that when we talked on the phone I fretted endlessly about earthquakes.

I hugged him and watched him pull away from the curb in his yellow Mustang convertible. He was a long way from motorcycles now. We had agreed that tomorrow we would spend the day together.

California (Northern California, at least) possesses the appearance of paradise. I forced myself not be taken in by appearances. I needed to be watchful and observant. Danger could be lurking almost anywhere.

For two days I kept my eyes open, scrutinizing every face we passed, observing gestures. I put my powers of observation onto full alert, particularly when he introduced me to his friends.

Max, a Nigerian Jean-Louis often spoke to me about, was a courtly and kind man. He was incredibly tall.

Shirley, a pretty young woman with blond hair and a slightly affected squint, seemed obsessed with her appearance. She and Jean-Louis played tennis. It was clear their relationship went no deeper.

Audrey, a plump young woman with a very sweet disposition, informed me within a minute of our acquaintance that she was in love with a guitarist in a jazz fusion band. From what I could tell, Jean-Louis was a sort of brother to her, a soul willing to listen to her tales of infatuation.

Amanda was a different matter. I knew that she had slept with my son the minute I saw them exchange a conspiratorial look. She was beautiful, with Sharon Stone–like looks, but I found her lacking mystique — the case for so many American women. She was too tanned, too blond, too — how can I put it? — self-assured. I had a hard time imagining her cooking up a plot against us.

The only person who seemed even mildly suspicious was Gregory, who lived on the same floor as my son. He was gay and sported a long beard. He had a faraway look, and indeed was very involved in spiritual matters — a channel for voices, he said, a medium for souls from the Other Side. "I'm a kind of phone line between the living and the dead," he confided to me (nearly making me burst out laughing). "Yesterday I put an old woman in touch with a man who lived four thousand years ago. The man used my mouth to say that his spirit would come to her and help her leave her mortal coil, so that she might join with eternals."

Good heavens, I thought.

"See, the key to it," he added in hushed tones, "is that they had once been lovers in the lost city of Atlantis."

Gregory's sole purpose in life was to help people find their Disembodied Superior Self, to better enable them to make the astral journey. He added with dismay that he couldn't convince Jean-Louis of this, though it was clear that my son was an ancient soul.

The more I listened to him, the more I realized that Gregory was more a figure of pity than an object for suspicion. I was quickly persuaded that his plans for "holistic global consciousness" didn't conceal some Machiavellian scheme.

Despite all the cant about the spirits of enlightenment, all these leafy ideologies, all the talk about the rejuvenating powers of certain kinds of water, all the otherworldly premonitions about the coming of the Age of Spiritual Enlightenment, and all sorts of other neosixties hogwash, I found Berkeley quite a healthy place on the whole. All this self-indulgence took place in a pleasant climate, where vigorous exercise and clean living were the strongest cults of all. Jean-Louis seemed to be living a life that was both healthy and sane. He jogged every morning, played tennis twice a week, and he studied hard.

Indeed, the strongest impression I got about my son from this trip was how much more mature he seemed. How absurd was the idea that he was caught up in some shady business. I decided to relax and enjoy our last day together. We had a picnic beneath the sequoias, California's most venerable treasures.

And so it was with a light heart that I went to the Young Museum in San Francisco to examine the Le Nain painting.

The central question, of course, was which Le Nain were we talking about here? There are three — Mathieu, Antoine, and Louis, all brothers — just as there are three furies, three graces, three kings, three witches in *Macbeth,* three little pigs, three cardinal virtues, and three fates. Their lives are a complete mystery. We don't even know the year of their births. Le Nain (which means "the dwarf") is, metaphorically, a three-headed, six-handed creature. The question was, which of the three painted which painting? Often when they signed their works they used a first name, but followed by a question mark, because they collaborated. Deciding which was whose was a dicey affair, even for experts like myself.

Who indeed is responsible for all those magnificent portraits of country folk, immortalized in their misery and despair? Those pictures were thorns in the side of Louis XIII and his cronies at the court of the Louvre. Somber indictments of aristocratic excess. The three dwarves painted to express their identification with the poor, to demand bread for them. Some dared to call the paintings vulgar and ridiculous. I find they possess a poignant majesty.

The Le Nain I was to look at was part of the country folk series, though the size of the canvas was smaller than usual — somewhat along the lines of *Visiting Grandmothers.*

It had the same dark shades of browns and spots of color, the same stiffness and self-consciousness.

The tests done on the work appeared to confirm its authenticity. Microscopic and spectrometric analyses provided further proof. But some lingering doubt remained; to put it to rest the Young's curators wanted an outside opinion.

Despite the test results thus far, the painting was on the borderline between being a true work and a fake. A large number of paintings in the world today exist in such a state of limbo.

Experts such as myself are called in to provide some transcendental truth that either will save them or damn them. When we cannot provide this service, we become the objects of scorn. The pressure to decide matters definitively is enormous.

The truth is that sometimes certainty is simply not possible. What mistakes have been committed in the name of "gut reaction"! Innocent people have been put into prisons, and "masterpieces" hung on the walls of the Louvre or the Met. So many errors of attribution! Think of the now legendary *Hurdy-Gurdy Player*, which has been attributed, respectively, to Murillo, Zurbarán, Velázquez, Rizzi, Strozzi, Herrera the Elder, and Mayno. These days it is considered the work of either Georges Dumesnil de La Tour or "Unknown."

A relative matter, this business of attribution. Determining whether the painting in question was a true Le Nain would complicate matters enough, given that there are three possible fathers.

I was shown the painting and went to work: I gazed at

it, sniffed it, tasted it, and scrutinized the contrasts in the planes of color. I felt a curious sensation of detachment. The painting looked perfect, but it didn't breathe. True masterpieces transport you inside their world. Not this one. There were, moreover, some suspicious-looking cracks.

The instant I can tell something is a copy I am repelled, forced by a deep feeling of revulsion to turn away from the work. I detest fakery in all of its forms. If I am sure of my opinion, I will not withhold it. I am one of the few in my field to be so blunt, I believe. It is a matter of integrity. I find it extraordinary that others can be so casual about the truth.

I remember a conversation I had with a historian, a renowned academic, who, among other things, was extremely tolerant.

"Really, Charles," he said to me once. "Think about it for a moment. Where does creation start? Picasso himself said that the light of a painting always gives rise to another painting. And Pascal teased Montaigne years after Montaigne's death about how much he borrowed from Plutarch. Aren't we all plagiarists in some sense?"

I asked him if all those wonderful turns of phrase I'd read in his last book were really his, or if he had "borrowed" them from some other source.

The curator at the Young Museum was nearly in tears by the time I had finished rendering my judgment. I spent a good deal of time consoling him, then left for the airport. I was flying to Los Angeles to visit the celebrated Griffith Institute, which works closely with the Getty Conservation Institute in Marina del Rey and the Getty Museum in Malibu. Griffith was one of the few laboratories I was not familiar with that was devoted to pictorial study.

The visit was very edifying. What remarkable progress has been made in the study of painting since Wilhelm Conrad Röntgen first X-rayed a canvas in 1895! Like all art historians, I am deeply appreciative of the gifts scientific analysis has given us. Machines see things the human eye cannot. By bringing invisible images to the surface, and revealing the stages of artistic creation — sketches, paint-overs, second thinking — photographic techniques, radiography, and microchemical analysis, to name a few, have been of indispensable help. I am the first to pay them homage.

The Griffith was at the cutting edge of this kind of technology. The director, bursting with pride, showed me all his marvelous equipment. I told him how impressed I was by everything, which elated him.

My words inspired him to take me into his confidence.

"I have something remarkable to tell you. We are at this very moment in the process of analyzing a large work attributed to Claude Lorrain. You of all people must realize what this means. An unknown masterpiece!"

This was stunning news indeed.

"Where is the painting from?" I managed.

"I'm afraid I can't say. All that I can tell you is that the first results were very, very positive. They came from the Oxford Institute."

Ah, yes. The Oxford Institute. I remembered meeting Jane Caldwell at a symposium a year earlier. A striking woman, though very emotional. The fame of her laboratory was growing. One of these days, I thought, I am going to have to go and pay it a visit.

I told the Griffith director I was intrigued by the news, and would await further developments.

3

My trip to California had set the world to rights. On the plane taking me home to Paris, I relived each moment with Jean-Louis, who — to my delight — had told me he would be coming back to France at Christmas. That was a mere three months off. I would find the tree ornaments, I would shop for gifts. And I would work in peace — and with peace of mind.

I took advantage of everything Air France's first class had to offer — champagne, caviar, foie gras, Bordeaux. I had refound my taste for life, and the appetite followed.

Relief reconnected me to my surroundings. Before, everything had left me feeling distracted or bored. Daily news seemed irrelevant. Now I could read the newspaper with gusto. It was all so compelling — the latest elections in France, developments in the Middle East, the stock market. Most compelling of all was the possibility that a lost Lorrain painting had been found.

I found myself looking with interest at the woman

sitting across the aisle from me. There was, I found, something very appealing about her. Her head was leaning to one side, affording a view of what looked like an extremely comely earlobe.

I have always found ears sensual parts of the female body, whether chaste ears, white and fine, or voluptuous ears with fleshy lobes, such as the ones you find in a Toulouse-Lautrec portrait.

The pearl-like specimens belonging to my neighbor on the plane made me want to nuzzle them. Ever since the death of Sophie, I have had no real love life, though now and again the dull roots will stir, set off by something small usually — a smell, a freckle, an ear. Desire is bittersweet, for I am always reminded by these twinges that I can never again share them with Sophie.

Before Sophie, love was to me what it is to so many men: a form of exchange. These dalliances poison the soul, I am sure of it. Worse, they instill boredom.

Sophie had tumbled into my life on the eve of my fortieth birthday, by the purest of chance and the most unlikely of places: a museum devoted exclusively to Chinese puzzles, located in a suburb of Paris.

What first drew my attention to her was her laugh — the quality of it, the true joy it seemed to express. I turned my head to find its source and found myself looking at dimpled cheeks and eyes the color of pine pitch, eyes alive with mischief.

She was with another young woman, and the two of them were giggling uncontrollably before an ivory *baguenaudier,* one of those games of dexterity designed to drive one crazy.

Our eyes met. From that moment onward my one over-riding fear in the world was losing her. I followed the two women out. Luck was with me. When we got to the museum's exit, it was pouring rain. I was standing with them in the entryway. They were debating how to get to the train station without getting soaked. I offered to share my umbrella and then, throwing caution to the winds, invited them to join me at the café across the way. That way, I said, we could wait out the rain.

Before we had even finished our coffee I knew I wanted her. I wanted to live with her, I wanted her to have my children. My love was immediate and authentic. I had found the real thing.

By the time we parted company that day, I knew everything I needed to about her: that she was single, lived alone, and composed music. I even found out where she lived.

The next day I hurried over to the corner where her building was located. I had no particular plan in mind. I suppose I simply hoped that "by accident" we would meet. A fierce thunderstorm was brewing. Walking beneath the windows, I heard someone making beautiful sounds, sounds that seemed to come from some other universe. A piano. I found the spot where I could hear it best and stood there, transfixed.

In my mind now the music I heard merged with that late-summer thunderstorm, expressing the eternal combat between light and dark, between power and grace. Whoever had created that sound was not one of those poor scribblers who crowd contemporary music with atonal, passionless sounds. It was her music. It was she. She was becoming a work of art to me, a painting broken free, gloriously free, of its frame.

I would have waited a week in that summer storm, there on that corner. But the heavens smiled. The rain stopped, the music stopped, and Sophie emerged from her apartment. I ran around the corner, turned around, buried my nose in a book, and rounded the corner again — two steps ahead of her. Oops!

"Well, well," I said, sounding as casual as I could, "isn't this a surprise!"

She burst out laughing. "Sorry I'm late. I was practicing scales. So, shall we be off?"

I looked at her, confused, but nodded.

An hour later, we were listening to a student of Benjamin Britten's playing a very cosmic version of *The Clocks of Lakmé* on a Moog synthesizer. Our fingers met.

Afterward, she invited me to her apartment. She had already prepared a lunch for two.

Sophie never admitted that she'd seen me from the window, nor that she had planned the whole thing. I never asked her.

Three months later, she said "I do" at the Hotel de Ville. Nine months after that I was holding her hand in a dismal birthing room. At 10:29 in the morning one Sunday in September, we had Jean-Louis.

Over the months our lives blossomed. What had I done to deserve this happiness? She composed sonatas, Jean-Louis grew, and I worked on my projects. Our life was a priceless work of art, a magic circle. I had nothing left to wish for.

"Such happiness cannot last," my grandmother would have said.

It didn't. Faces, portraits, tell everything. We pretended, Sophie and I, that she was not that ill: it was just mastitis.

The test her doctor wanted to run was a routine mammography, the sort that women take regularly. I nonetheless decided to go with her.

While the technician was developing the X rays, the doctor showed us an echograph and a scintilloscope, diagnostic equipment that was, as I remarked, not so different from the machines that analyze works of art. I remember having drawn parallels between the ways of detecting anomalies of the breast and those used to find a composition hidden beneath the surface of Rembrandt's *Portrait of a Young Man* — in that case a woman leaning over a cradle.

Suddenly the technician ended the conversation and said in a perceptibly different tone, "OK, fine. The X rays are very clear. Dr. Bernard will get these results the day after tomorrow, at the very latest."

The following morning Dr. Bernard called. He wanted to examine Sophie and to run some more tests. A simple biopsy, that's all. A week later, when the results had arrived, we went to see him.

Sophie would need an operation, he told us, and as soon as possible. Behind the carefully chosen words and couched phrases I could make out the words "cancer," "chemo," and "radiology."

The operation was set for three days hence. We spent two days shuttling between fear and hope.

After the operation, it was all too clear that Sophie had breast cancer. It had metastasized into her liver. Small-cell cancer. The swiftest and most terrible of all.

Watching her fade away was like watching a great work disintegrate. Soon all that was left was a sketch from which all color had seeped away. Then even it was gone from view.

Jean-Louis, a mere toddler, kept me from giving in to terror and despair. With time I experienced a sort of rebirth, the kind that comes when the heart, wrung dry, finds another reason to live.

I began loving Jean-Louis like a mother and a father. Sophie's love for him had become part of my love for him. Through him, she lived in me. Sometimes the sensation of her presence is physical. She is sitting on the bed. I can feel the weight of her head on my shoulder. I can caress the folds of her dress while talking to her, even smell her perfume.

Slowly, brush stroke by brush stroke, my life after her death regained some of its fullness. I had two missions, two guiding lights: Jean-Louis and art. Everything else meant nothing. I had few friends, no hobbies. I concentrated only on what was essential, on what lay at the heart of my existence. With that kind of focus, I almost had no choice but to become famous.

The disdain with which I treated my growing renown made me all the more renowned.

I became France's best-known expert on seventeenth-century painting by dint of sheer hard work, intuition, and a steady eye. "Only the eyes of the master can really see," says La Fontaine. I not only learned to see, I learned how to listen to art.

I thought again about this mysterious, recently surfaced Lorrain. Eventually the final pronouncement of its authenticity would be mine to give — or withhold.

4

The minute I returned home from the airport I discovered a fourth white envelope in my pile of mail. The postmark was Brussels.

Instinctively, I ran out onto the sidewalk, believing I might see whomever had mailed it lurking there. When I got into the elevator with my luggage I half expected to find someone there. I felt watched.

Once inside my apartment I double-bolted the door and pulled close the curtains. My heart was beating erratically.

Three times I picked up the phone with the intention of calling the police. Three times I put the phone back in its cradle. Meanwhile the envelope remained as it was. I held it in my moist hands for fifteen minutes, then finally opened it.

A photo of Jean-Louis at a picnic under a tree with friends.

There was something else in the envelope. A yellowed newspaper clipping that read "Mysterious Death of

Onassis's Son." Part of an article recounting the famous plane accident followed.

My chest tightened in panic. The threat was real now. The photographs were but suggestions, intimations. The clipping was a direct threat.

I felt as I had the morning after Sophie's death — desperately alone, teetering on the brink of some gaping pit. My thoughts spun. I needed something to keep me from falling.

Remain rational, I told myself. What would the police have done? Looked for fingerprints on the envelope or on the photograph.

I found some pencil lead and ground it into a fine graphite dust, spread it across the back of the envelope, blew on it, then did the same thing with the photo and the clipping.

The envelope revealed two or three muddy-looking fingerprints, which I knew must belong either to the concierge or to me. In any case, what would I have done had I found someone's fingerprint? Gone to the police and asked them if it belonged to some criminal? The whole idea was absurd.

I called a photographer. He told me that it was impossible to determine where a standard roll of Kodak film had been developed, unless there were a name or address on the back of the print. Of course there wasn't. There was only a series of numbers.

"The date of manufacture and the date of development are usually fairly close together," the photographer told me. "Film doesn't keep very long. It loses its sensitivity to light."

I'd learned nothing. The person who'd photographed Jean-Louis had probably bought the film this year, and probably in the United States. The back of the photo read "This paper manufactured by Kodak."

I was thrown back into despair, into a realm of utter help-lessness where thoughts ran riot. I'm told the best thing is to let it all wash over you, rather than trying to stare it down.

There was nothing to do but wait. Batten down the hatches and point my prow into the wind. I would have to end up somewhere.

Had I been the one in danger, this would have been easy. The press clipping proved that it was my son's life that was being threatened. I was no Onassis, of course, though it was probably public knowledge that I was well off. That I would have enough cash to pay a ransom. I thought of famous cases of kidnapping. Some victims were released after payment. Most were killed. Plenty of kidnappings went unreported. Families quietly paid what was asked of them by mafioso types.

Perhaps it wasn't money that they were after. What does a blackmailer want besides money? A deed, a title, a promise, a signature, a painting, a jewel, a secret formula, a manu-script? Anything was possible. I was dealing with a criminal and a sadist, someone who knew what was most precious to me in the world.

That meant someone who knew me — a relative, a neighbor, a colleague, a friend. Someone nearby, watching me, playing with me, teasing me. Hating me.

Having spied upon my son, this monster would not sud-denly stop. He would neutralize me by forcing me to soak in my own fear. He would contact me, probably by phone. Perhaps he would come to the front door. Or send a telegram. I needed to stay home and stay alert, eyes looking both outward — watching others, and inward — watching me, to keep myself from going mad.

There are people who draw strength from the direst of circumstances. I do not count myself among them. I was completely out of my depth. My mind was like a wheel spinning in mud. I was skating. Every image my mind formed sent me skidding. Every effort to think only dragged me further into misery.

What could I hold on to? The phone. The only thing I could do was call Jean-Louis. It was six in the morning in Berkeley, but too bad. He had told me to call when I got back to Paris to tell him I'd arrived safely.

By the second ring I knew that he wasn't going to answer. I knew that from the tone of the phone's ring. It sounded as if it were ringing in a void. Jean-Louis hadn't bought an answering machine, so it would keep ringing. Finally, I hung up and dialed again. Maybe I'd dialed the wrong number. No, of course not. I hung up. All I could hear was a rumbling in my ears.

That is perhaps the worst moment of all — the moment when tragedy and sorrow are upon you, and there is nothing you can do to stop them. You stand and wait, passive, resigned, doomed.

I stared terrifiedly at the phone, hoping it would ring, hoping it wouldn't. I unplugged it and sat in silence.

Something was ringing somewhere. Not the phone. The doorbell? I found I was unable to move. Danger may have been waiting for me on the threshold, but it took more strength than I could summon to face it.

The bell rang a second time. This time, in a sort of spasm, I ran to the door and placed my ear against it, my heart pounding — then, with a jerk, I pulled it open.

There I found not unthinkable horror but daily life —

in the form of a messenger from my publishing house. He was delivering the proofs of my latest book. I managed to smile at him and scrawl my signature onto a piece of paper.

I was calmer when I closed the door. The interruption gave me some detachment. A voice somewhere inside was telling me that I was still myself.

Then, perhaps following from that detachment, I was overwhelmed by outrage and by anger. Someone was trying to push me over the edge. Enough! I'd had enough! It was time to turn things around.

Someone was setting a trap for me? All right! I would set one right back. Someone was threatening me? Fine. I would go straight at him. Someone wanted me to break down? Surprise! I would break *him* down. Someone was baring his teeth at me? He would get bitten. Someone thought he had me down? Never.

I had to sketch out a plan. These photographs were precursors to murder — either mine or my son's or both.

Feeling resolved, I plugged the phone back in and opened my address book. My first determination was to come up with a list of suspects. Who could wish such evil upon me?

Two hours later I had come up with a list. On it were three people.

First was Egon Adalbert, a German colleague I had humiliated on a number of occasions. Six months before, in fact, I had lacerated Adalbert publicly about a Dürer imitation he had insisted, wrongheadedly, was authentic. My language had been a little strong. Actually, when I examined the piece in question, I found it very handsome. It had been done by an ingenious copier named Luca Giordano. Giordano amused himself by concealing his signature in his works the way children's book illustrators conceal faces in trees. I had had little difficulty in exposing Adalbert's ridiculous supposition.

Had someone done the same to me, I too might have felt murderous rage.

Second on my list was Michel Calmette, my financial planner. Calmette and I had known each other since grade school, and he had heartily despised me his whole life. Why? God knows. It started with some childish resentment and kept growing. He was of that species of humanity constitutionally envious of everyone else. He had become quite a successful stockbroker, but nothing had changed between us. My professional success exasperated him. I enjoyed rubbing his nose in it from time to time. This was an old game between us, going back years. Calmette was basically a good-hearted fellow, and, in his own particular, bilious way, loyal.

My third suspect was Frederic Silberman. Now here was a piece of work. He was suspected (and rarely prosecuted) of all sorts of thievery, every manner of trickery. Silberman was a professional and highly successful fraud. He was a parasite who fed off the art world, having already fed off other fields and then moved on. The world was his stage and his only pleasure was in acting out every part he could.

To Silberman, duplicity was the highest form of self-expression. In his way he was quite an artist. He had been, in turn, a lawyer, a psychiatrist, a restaurateur, a management consultant, and a diplomat — changing his name and credentials as the role demanded.

At one point Silberman was a conman at a casino. He

got people to bet against him. He was arrested and banned for life from all casinos and gambling establishments in Europe. No matter: he moved on to other schemes.

He had sold small swatches of a shirt he maintained had belonged to Rudolph Valentino. For a while he shopped phony Louis XV cabinets, replete with certificates of authenticity, around Geneva. He had gone into publishing, printing late works by known (and deceased) writers, claiming the manuscripts had been discovered in a trunk.

Lately he had been pretending to be an art dealer, and was involved, I felt sure, in all sorts of dubious deals. He claimed to find masterpieces — not all of them were fakes, actually — and then sold them at the Dompierre Gallery in Paris. He had exhibited three handsome seventeenth-century fakes at the Wright-Hepburn gallery in London. There was talk at the time that they had been painted by a mysterious and highly gifted copier, examples of whose works had not yet fallen into my hands. He was apparently enormously gifted. A Hungarian, I believe.

You might wonder why a distinguished art historian such as myself had anything at all to do with a shady character like Silberman. The answer, truthfully, is that contact with such people is inevitable — as inevitable as a corrupt clergyman in the Age of Enlightenment. He turned up everywhere — at auctions, openings, exhibits, lectures. Every time he saw me he greeted me like his oldest and dearest friend.

I confess that I found him amusing and distracting. He knew his pretenses were a joke on the rest of the world. Besides, every time I saw him he had fresh gossip and new information. I took whatever he told me with a grain of salt, of course; everything he said or did was inspired by self-serving motives. Using hidden microphones he taped conversations he had with people.

"I am a voyeur of life," he told me once. "I love to observe hidden emotions. I love finding weak spots."

Weak spots. I wondered about that now. That sort of motivation made him a prime suspect. Perhaps too prime a suspect. The classic red herring?

Besides, what possible motivation could Silberman have to torture me? To uncover the agonizing truth behind my mask of civility and calm? Did he want me to authenticate something? This I doubted. Blackmailing me would not have been Silberman's style.

All these vague suspicions and cloudy motives. No hard proof of anything.

The entirety of that terrible day was spent trying to establish some kind of basis, however far-fetched, for an investigation. Throughout it, I must say I felt very much alive. Every nerve tingled. In this frame of mind, the least thing can suddenly seem like a mortal threat. Sounds become amplified and ominous: someone sweeping in the hallway, distant footsteps, a car's brakes squealing in the street, the muted thrum of someone's stereo.

By the time night had fallen, I had tried, in vain, to call Jean-Louis twenty times at least. Why in God's name hadn't I bought him an answering machine? My fear was alive, voraciously alive. My agony was acute. Despite all the resolutions I'd made that morning, I abandoned myself to fear. There is nothing worse than that.

Staggering into the bedroom, I collapsed onto my bed and fell into a troubled sleep.

I dreamt I was in the street, looking around wildly for a phone booth so that I could call Jean-Louis. When I found one, and tried feverishly to dial his number, the buttons cracked and crumbled to the ground like rotten teeth. I got down on all fours and tried to pick them up and stick them back on, but they kept slipping between my fingers. Finally, just when I thought I'd done it, another one was missing. When I found it, and began desperately to push it, it dissolved into marshmallow beneath my finger.

I awoke with a start, sweating profusely yet chilled to the bone. I cast my eyes around the room, expecting to see some horrific sight. I heard someone groan. It was me — I had groaned. Tears were streaming down my cheeks.

I went to the window and opened it wide. Morning was dawning, beautiful but chill. Paris was still there, spread out against the crystal and cloudless sky.

For a second I was prepared to find solace in this view, when a crow suddenly swooped down and landed on the ledge of my balcony. A bad sign, this angular, ungainly bird, this harbinger of evil tidings and unanswerable questions.

I realized, with the clarity of the growing dawn, that I would have to watch myself carefully, or else fall deeply, irrevocably perhaps, into paranoia.

5

nguish. Hate. Rage. Fear. Confusion. Most of all, confusion. On the dawn of this new day, where was I to start?

There was always my work, my professional evaluations — those page proofs, which my publisher expected me to finish going over by mid-October. That left me with barely two weeks to reread what had taken me years of painstaking work.

The book was called *The Last Works of the Greatest Painters, or, The Magnificent Trembling of Age*. The subtitle was from Chateaubriand, who, while discussing *The Deluge*, one of Poussin's final works, was reminded of "something letting go." The paintings, he said, showed "the hand of an old man."

Poussin was well acquainted with tremors of the hand. He wrote about them in his last letters, in which he complains of "the infirmity of my trembling hand, which will no longer do my bidding."

He was suffering from Parkinson's disease. How I had tried to find the right way to express his tragic struggle for control.

An artist's final work very often marks the advent of something new. My book argued that only at the end of his life was Poussin finally beginning to express his true self. This is precisely what Corot suggested on the eve of his own death: "I perceive things as I never have before," he wrote. "Suddenly it seems to me that not until now have I known how to paint the sky."

Themistocles and countless others have often said that man takes his leave of life when he is finally and truly ready to do so.

There was nothing ennobling about the shaking of my own hand, however. As I read over the proofs I was shocked at what I found. My reflections about these twilight works now appeared as confused as the words I was spewing out to express them. Rather than holding to a central theme, I was spinning my rhetorical wheels. It seemed to me, as I reread the pages, that they were crammed with febrile, flighty metaphors.

My eyesight had also changed. I looked at things differently. Studying the various reproductions scattered across my desk, all I could see were dark and evil omens. In van Gogh's *Church at Auvers,* a wonderful painting, my eyes focused on the crows with wings black as night.

In *The Deluge,* my eyes riveted on the drowning man, seen extending his arm helplessly and hopelessly toward a sky streaked with lightning. Then on the shipwreck, the black rocks, the bolt of lightning splitting the darkened sky.

Death, in everything and everywhere.

I was descending into madness. What was there to stop me? That silly list of suspects? Adalbert, Calmette, Silberman. I repeated them over and over like mantras.

Adalbert. Where would I find him? At an auction, of course.

Putting on my coat, I hurried to Drouot's, Paris's premier auction house. I knew I would find him there. On that particular Monday, they were selling one of the thousands upon thousands of "authentic" Corots floating about in the world.

He was indeed there, in the company of a German client. He looked nervous. The sale had put him into a full sweat. He clearly knew the thing was a fake. That tic he had of shrugging one shoulder was more pronounced than usual.

How flabby his cheeks looked. I'd never noticed that before, and I found it slightly revolting. He hurried toward me, his hand extended in greeting. A descriptive adjective for the man came to mind: "servile." He was one of the most unctuously servile and cowardly men I had ever met.

I became aware that I had become suspicious and ungenerous. Perhaps the time had come for me to let this side of my character speak for me. Perhaps it would lead me out of this mess.

We chatted for a few minutes, then he was called away. Nothing he said raised any suspicions. He seemed his normal, servile self. He didn't even mention the matter of the Dürer.

Frustrated, I went home. I had barely closed the door when the phone rang. It was Calmette, my banker and second suspect. A strange coincidence, I thought, his calling at that particular moment. We rarely talked.

"Charles old man, so sorry to bother you, but I wanted to let you know that the fluctuations in interest rates will do a little temporary damage to your financial portfolio."

What a moment to discuss this! This was Calmette through and through. As if I could have cared in the slightest about long-term interest rates!

"Your overseas investments have experienced rather heavy losses. The Asian market, you know. But this is not the moment to think of selling them."

I found his commiseration a little oily. He was enjoying giving me bad news. I could tell he was goading me because I had lost a little money.

"My dear Michel," I said in as cavalier a manner as I could manage, "this is of no importance whatsoever. I foresee no need for liquidity in the coming months."

My reaction seemed to deflate him a little. He explained that it would nonetheless be wise to stay in the Asian market. Things were bound to look up.

Asian markets. What did I care? But when he told me that he himself had just returned from Japan, where he had opened a branch office, I listened carefully. Calmette was many things, but he was no liar. I believed he really had just returned from Japan.

This meant that he could not have sent the photographs.

Then, after hanging up the phone, I remembered there used to be a dealer in postcards who made extra money by offering to have letters or cards sent from anywhere in the world — making the recipient believe that the sender had actually been there.

No, that was a ridiculous idea. I had to take Calmette off the list.

I decided to search out my third suspect, Silberman, so I went down to the street to hail a cab and promptly tripped on the sidewalk. If I hadn't managed to grab hold of a lamppost I would certainly have fallen and might have broken my leg.

What a silly, stupid thing to do. My son was in danger and needed me. Were something to happen to me, were I immobilized for some reason, or became sick, I wouldn't be able to face the crisis ahead. I reminded myself that I was after all sixty-two years old, no longer a young man. Life at that age is contingent. Several of my friends were already buried in Père-Lachaise cemetery, final resting place for so many luminaries. The strain on my heart and my nerves these last few weeks was severe. I was feeling decidedly fragile.

Hobbling on one leg, I hailed a cab and collapsed into the backseat. My ankle had begun to swell and was throbbing with pain. Probably sprained. Another sign that the world was against me.

By this point I had begun seeing signs everywhere. Every nerve and hair was alert to them, miniature antennae alive to the slightest sound, the faintest odor. The smallest things unnerved me: a chair sticking out, a dripping faucet, the shape of a cloud.

I felt the constant urge to check and recheck everything: the oven gas, the chain on my front door, the window locks, my wallet. I did this without thinking. I was also fretting ceaselessly about my appearance, like some insecure teenager worried whether his zipper is up. I suppose my mind was trying to distract me from greater worries.

When I walked into Silberman's gallery, my first reaction

was that the world had gone mad, stark, raving, and completely mad. The paintings hanging on the walls were brutal and shocking. Huge clashes of colors, scenes of flagellation and sadistic devastation, bodies writhing in agony.

It took me a moment to see what they actually were: modern depictions of Saint Sebastian's martyrdom. How, I wondered, could anyone massacre color to quite that extent?

The gallery's owner, Richard Dompierre, stood in the middle of these so-called works of art, barking orders and clapping his hands. The pathetic old queen.

"Ah, Charles! My dear, dear friend," he cried, nearly melting into my arms when I asked for news of Silberman.

Distraught, Dompierre told me that Silberman had spent the last three weeks in jail. He stood accused of fraud, knowingly trying to sell a forgery. It was all a monstrous frame-up perpetrated by enemies and competitors. By locking up his closest friend and business associate they were trying to put him, Dompierre, out of business.

Calmette and Silberman had alibis. I was back to Adalbert.

I briefly offered Dompierre my sympathies and hobbled out of the gallery feeling depressed. How ridiculous all my suspicions were. They were getting me nowhere. I was a pathetic old fool unable to help his own son. All I was good for was pontificating.

Good heavens. I would be late for my weekly lecture at the College.

When I reached the lecture hall, the eyes of fifty restless students trained on me — young, leering, vibrant faces. What had I to teach them? I was suddenly seized with the desire to fling up my hands and run away. Couldn't they see I wasn't who they thought I was? What was the point of chatting on about art? It was so pointless and so silly.

Nonetheless, my lecture that day was — I must say — quite brilliant. I discussed the symbolic rites and rituals frequently involved in artistic creation. My anxieties must have given me a nervous energy, for my remarks sparkled. Afterward, curiously, I felt a little better. So did my ankle.

Back home, I did three very small things that helped reestablish order in my life, restore a semblance of peace: I cleaned up a bit, opened the curtains to let in some light, and put on a Vivaldi concerto. The best medicine of all was when Jean-Louis called, sounding as happy and full of life as ever. For a moment my fears dissolved.

The next morning, when I went down to get the mail, they returned in full force. With each step, my heart tightened. I looked with terror at the little pile of mail in my box, like a sick old man staring at a letter containing his test results.

It was there of course. The envelope. Postmarked Oslo.

I attempted to control my breathing. I climbed the stairs slowly and deliberately, and opened the door to my apartment without haste. Then I sat in my chair and calmly slit open the letter, as if it were a mailing from a charitable society. All this took an enormous effort of will.

I drew out the photograph of Jean-Louis. He was captured jogging through some beautiful countryside. You could see the sea far off in the distance, in the middle distance were towering trees, and, on the left-hand side, some large rocks. The photo had the composition of a painting, I noted. It was slightly overexposed.

I was forcing myself to maintain my composure, when something in the picture made me cry out in rage and fear. On Jean-Louis's forehead, exactly between his eyes, was a small point of red light, perfectly round and precise. My God. A laser sight from a high-powered rifle, the sort that can kill from two hundred yards away. That was what made that sort of light. Practically every Hollywood action film these days featured them.

Part of me knew that this idea was crazy, but the supposition was enough to unhinge me. The word "laser" echoed over and over in my brain, followed by images of . . . of — I couldn't bear it — images of horror. A voice was telling me something.

"Terrible forces are at work here."

A voice? Whose voice? Where? I was inside my apartment. Was somebody else also inside? I ran down the hall into the kitchen, then into my bedroom. I was dimly aware that I was throwing open drawers in my dresser — looking for what I now have no idea — then collapsed in a heap on my bed and broke down in sobs.

I was a complete mess, a creature of hysteria and madness, alternating moans and prayers and incoherent cries of anguish. I implored God, I implored my invisible enemy. Had I known who my tormentor was I would have run to him and prostrated myself. I, Charles Vermeille!

For weeks I had been caught in the black magic of despair. Nothing made sense but everything was ominous, and fanatically, terribly meaningful. I grasped at straws. It was all like Kafka, or Émile Zola.

Émile Zola. My apartment building was located on rue Vineuse, which was the setting Zola had chosen for that grim melodrama, *A Page of Love*. The novel is about a good woman whose heart is supposedly taken over by "evil."

It all starts with the death of her child. Suddenly this had deep resonance in my soul.

I ran to my library to find a copy of that dreary little book. It had been years since I'd read it, but I was sure I had one somewhere. I found it.

One never reads the same book twice. That is a simple and profound truth. It is not the words that have changed, but the person reading them. I had hardly remarked on the novel the first time I read it. On that day, however, every sentence seemed a reflection of my predicament. That poor woman! She falls in love with a married man, and for this she must endure horrific punishment. The child must die.

What did that mean? Was I to be the cause of my son's death? Instead of rooted in a father's love, were my feelings for him rooted in destructive selfishness? Did my sin lie in believing Jean-Louis was mine alone?

I got up and opened the window. Much about the city had changed since Zola's day, of course, but on that night his description in the book matched what I saw: "Paris, illuminated by a luminous cloud, the fiery blast of a furnace hovering over the city, produced by the groaning lives that it devours and spews out as fire and brimstone, like the clouds of smoke and steam that gather around the mouth of a volcano."

I snapped the book shut and picked up the photograph of Jean-Louis, the most recent one. Something strange was stirring within me, struggling to rise to the surface of my consciousness. Memories, images. I could neither stop them nor explain them. A countryside; trees looking as if they had been painted, leaf by leaf; expanses of sky; a small waterfall and — over on the left — a fallen tree in the foreground; a play of light.

I knew this vision.

The scenes evaporated like bubbles, like words that form on the tip of the tongue and then dissolve. I was left with a feeling of unease and uncanny strangeness. Déjà vu.

"Columns. Where are the columns?" a voice within me asked.

I went into my study and put the photo under ultraviolet light, then pored over every square inch, convinced now that I would find something to help me understand. No, nothing. I decided to enlarge it on a screen with a projector. I stood in front of it for half an hour, forcing myself to look at it not as a photograph of my son, but as a composition, as a work of art.

I focused all my attention on that tiny point of light. Could it be a reflection from a mirror — a watch crystal, or a magnifying glass, perhaps — made to look like a laser point? For that to be so, my son would have had to have been a willing participant, holding his pose while the reflection could be beamed on the point between his eyes.

That was not possible. It had to have been a reflection, an accident, a fluke. For the first time in hours, my breathing slowed.

Now that the point of light no longer drew all my attention, I began to look at the landscape around him, staring at it until my eyelids began to get heavy and the need to sleep overpowered me. I went into the bedroom and collapsed onto the bed fully clothed, and then fell into a deep sleep.

How many times since this whole miserable business

began I had been jolted from sleep, seized with a spasm that gripped my guts and set my throat on fire. I would barely make it into the bathroom to vomit into the sink, my whole body wracked with nausea.

Then, straightening up, I would look at my reflection in the mirror. I was a vision of horror in the dim morning light — gasping like a carp on a kitchen table, trying to take in large, milky gulps of air.

This time I awoke feeling refreshed. My body seemed to have rid itself of torpor and was preparing itself for combat — though with whom or with what I had no idea. I didn't feel threatened so much as challenged. I felt a sense of dark jubilation at what lay ahead.

Here was what I had realized: if someone were threatening me for some reason other than money, it was because they were afraid of me. I was the threat to them, not the other way around. What I was therefore experiencing was *their* fear — my system was reacting as if to a foreign body. The question was, why?

I felt I would soon learn the answer. Waiting was now not only the only thing to do, it was the only reasonable thing to do. Reason, at last, reason.

6

The following night I had the oddest dream. I was cleaning the sky and the trees in the Luxembourg Gardens with a sponge soaked in mercury chloride. I was trying to uncover an image of Jean-Louis. Instead appeared one of the three Arcadian shepherds in that famous painting by Poussin, the shepherd on bended knee in the right-hand side of the painting. He was pointing toward some Roman ruins in the background and saying, "Over there. Over there is where you should scrub. Can't you see it's filthy?"

I dreamt that I tried to make my way toward the ruins, but the wind was blowing hard against me and I couldn't reach them.

I woke with the sensation that I had been in touch with something deep in my subconscious. That I had found some kind of key.

The landscape, that strange dream, the Arcadian shepherd. Uniting them all was a distinct impression of déjà vu.

I was on the threshold of a mystery and the solution was inside me. I wasn't waiting for a phone call, or a telegram, or a knock at the door. No, I was waiting for . . . myself. What I was sensing was the approach of an answer, a dénouement. Danger is oddly less threatening when it is imminent.

For the first time in weeks I was able to keep down a little breakfast, and make at least a half-hearted stab at my old morning chess ritual.

I felt fit in body and mind, though more keenly alert than ever to signs and omens. But now I was enjoying puzzling over their meanings. They were auspicious. With almost childish relief I saw a crow land briefly on my balcony and then fly off, as if frightened. Several days before one had perched there for hours on end.

In the reproductions of all the final works by celebrated painters I had chosen for the *Magnificent Trembling of Age* I no longer saw only the memento mori, but a larger frame of reference, the greater and more life-affirming game of images within images, as in Lucas Cranach's *Melancholy,* where a large bay window opens onto a whole new picture.

My thinking had become magnetized, drawing to it thoughts and ideas like iron filings. For example, when examining a painting of Mary Magdalene by Jacques Bellange, who depicted her with her eyes lifted to the heavens, the name of a famous astrophysicist suddenly popped into my head. I had never met the man, but there his name was. I felt a desire to meet him.

The next morning I was reading a magazine and came across an interview with that same astrophysicist. The article featured a photograph of him, taken at his office. Behind his desk was a reproduction of Bellange's painting.

The coincidence was unnerving but fascinating. Why would I think of this astrophysicist? What did the Mary Magdalene have to do with any of this? Because her eyes were looking to the heavens?

Questions begot questions. I thought a great deal about my helpful Arcadian shepherd, and when I did I found both that my anxieties eased and that images and ideas started springing to mind. At first the sensation was exhilarating, but as time passed it became irritating and dizzying. It reminded me of the way one's head spins when one lies down after having had too much to drink.

It was in this state that I answered the phone when it rang at precisely five o'clock.

"May I please speak to Professor Vermeille?" asked a voice unknown to me, with a slight accent. Belgian, I guessed.

"This is he," I replied.

"Forgive me for disturbing you. My name is Quentin Van Nieuwpoort. Sir, I'm calling you because, well, I've got something that might interest you."

"You have my attention."

"It involves a painting by Claude Lorrain."

Good God, not another, I thought. In fact I very nearly hung up the phone, but politeness kept me from doing so.

"A painting that might be attributed to Lorrain. Is that what you mean?"

I had seen so many Lorrain copies in my time that I had long become used to disappointing dealers and collectors. Still, my response seemed not to have fazed this man.

"Believe me, Professor Vermeille, I am not wasting your

time. The painting has been declared authentic by both the Oxford Institute for Art Research and the Griffith Institute in Los Angeles. I have certificates. This is the real thing. Except — well — it lacks your conclusive opinion."

It was the painting I'd heard about in Los Angeles. After the Griffith's director had taken me into his confidence I'd gleaned more details about the painting in question from a friend at Sotheby's. I'd also looked through my own notes. Identifying the work had been easy, thanks to the painter's own *Libro di Veritá,* carefully conserved in the manuscript collection at the British Museum.

As I've mentioned, the *Libro* was essentially an inventory, in which Lorrain had himself patiently redrawn, in pen and wash, his entire oeuvre. He'd based the drawings on his working sketches. The *Libro* provided valuable information about the paintings: the dates and places of their genesis, the dimensions of the frames, the clients who had commissioned them, and even, in certain cases, the names of their eventual purchasers.

The work had to have been number six of the *Libro: Port Scene,* painted by the artist during his stay in Naples in 1636, and last seen in Scotland in the middle of the nineteenth century.

"Can you bring the work to me? I have everything I need to study it here in my home."

"Certainly. Tomorrow afternoon," replied Van Nieuwpoort. "Sotheby's is handling everything."

"Yes, fine. Then come tomorrow afternoon. Two o'clock, if that's all right." It was. I gave him my address.

I was very anxious to see the painting. No believer in miracles was Charles Vermeille, particularly when a Lorrain was involved, but I had never entirely given up hope that someday another one of his works would resurface.

My hands shook as I took my mail out of my box the next morning. While I was sorting through the stack of magazines and ads an envelope fell to the floor. I recognized it immediately. Mailed from Paris. I picked it up, then opened it.

The photograph showed Jean-Louis on a dock in San Francisco. He was leaning against the railing, looking pensively out into the bay. Behind him were the masts of sailboats. The water looked calm. The light came from the right, an autumnal light, giving everything a reddish glow. The mist on the horizon gave the photo a feeling of depth. The air seemed light.

What I had understood only unconsciously before now struck me full force.

The wooded landscape, the port. They were classic Lorrain subjects. This view of San Francisco had been photographed in such a way as to resemble his famous work *The Port of Ostia*. The parallel lay in the scale.

That was it. It was because of Claude Lorrain that my life was being terrorized. The port of San Francisco. *The Port of Ostia*. The port scene listed in the *Libro di Veritá*. The call from this mysterious Van Nieuwpoort. They were all linked. Behind this . . . thing, this monstrous thing that had brought me to my knees and bled me dry and nearly ripped my heart out, was a painting. A painting!

I nearly roared in anger. No revenge would suffice for what I had been put through. It would stay with me as long as I lived, and when I died I would take this hate with me.

I had never felt such raw hate, born of blood and love. It had a terrible power.

Thus did I await the arrival of this Belgian. At two o'clock that afternoon my doorbell rang. Van Nieuwpoort introduced himself and entered, accompanied by two Sotheby's employees carrying a wooden crate.

Van Nieuwpoort was a surprise to me. He had a great smile and an enormous red nose. I immediately found him endearing, even charming. He was a jowly, squirely man. His oval head and enormous mustache gave him the air of a country gentleman come to sell some cattle at a local fair. This was not a man capable of evil — not someone with a nose that had obviously been dipped so deeply into his country's malts and barleys. His handshake was firm and warm.

"I am indebted to you. Indebted to you! Seeing me on such short notice. You can guess I'm pretty impatient to show you my beauty! Not to doubt your opinion, of course, sir, but, well — ahem — the painting has been authenticated by two great institutes, and you know —"

I stopped him there, first in order to remind him of certain hard truths in these matters, and second so that I could contain my own mounting excitement at the idea of seeing this painting. I needed to stay sharp. Van Nieuwpoort seemed innocent enough, but somewhere someone was setting a trap.

"I must warn you, that doesn't mean very much," I said. "The world's museums are packed with forgeries authenticated by the best laboratories and the most highly qualified experts. You might remember the Van Meegeren Vermeers. Holland's most famous expert at the time, Abraham Bredius, was completely taken in by these forgeries. He even went so far as to pronounce *Pilgrims of Emmaus* Vermeer's finest work. Then there was Wolfgang Rohrich's fake Cranach, Otto Wacker's phony van Goghs —"

"Of course, Professor Vermeille, of course. But come, come. It's got to mean something that the painting is listed in that libro thing. Sketch number six, I'm told. Painted by the artist in 1636. He was staying in Naples."

My guess had been correct. The port scene. It was more than possible that this work was authentic. I struggled to conceal my excitement.

"That's still no guarantee," I cautioned. "Despite all the precautions taken to control the flood of forgeries that arose even during his own lifetime, Lorrain nonetheless remains among the most copied painters in the history of art. I'm sorry, I'm really not trying to sound so discouraging. Come, let's have a look at your painting."

While the Sotheby's employees were unpacking the painting, Van Nieuwpoort showed me the copies of the authenticating reports. He told me that the painting had been discovered in the attic of his great-uncle's manor, which he had inherited, along with all its paintings and furnishings.

Given the layers of dust that covered everything, and the date of the storage records, it seemed to have sat in that attic since the end of the last century. Van Nieuwpoort explained that his great-uncle had been a passionate hunter. Possibly he had bought the work in Scotland, where he went each year to shoot grouse. Unfortunately, however, no one had been able to find either the bill of sale or any papers verifying provenance among his great-uncle's effects.

Number six on the *Libro* had crossed the Channel and,

sometime around the middle of the nineteenth century, ended up in the collection of the Glasgow City Art Gallery.

All traces of the work vanished in 1882, though two large engravings and two copies of the painting survived. The best copy resides in the museum in Grenoble, bearing the inscription "1636, Naples." I had studied Lorrain's Naples period in minute detail.

The painting was unpacked. I helped place it on an easel I had prepared, then stood back to have a look.

I instantly recognized the master's technique, style, and hand. Everything about this work, at least at first glance, bespoke Lorrain — particularly the amplitude of the subject. The brush strokes were hard to see beneath the surface lacquer, but the overall impression was . . . stunning. As in the *Disembarkation of the Queen of Sheba* and other port scenes, a rising sun irradiated everything.

It was classic Lorrain. His use of light had been his greatest gift to painting. Radiating from the middle of the painting was the sun — not simply a decorative element but the work's heart and unifying force. All the colors and shades in the painting stood in relation to its centrality.

As was his custom, the artist had used both a brush and his hand to blend colors. I frequently found Lorrain's palmprints and fingerprints embedded in the texture of the sky, though the impressions were not clean enough to be used as a test for forgery.

The rising sun's rays gave the curved surface of a ruined Roman temple's long Corinthian columns a golden hue, while the old fort of Naples and the vessels anchored at the harbor's mouth were bathed in the clarity of morning light. Lorrain's technique was to combine realism — as in the depiction of the port's fortifications and the vessels at anchor — with mythical constructions. It was his way of underscoring the play of symbols. Reality is atemporal. The viewer's gaze is compelled to seek a more glorious horizon, and there to find the source of light that is the beginning and end of all spiritual quests.

"Well, professor?"

Concealing my enthusiasm was pointless.

"The painting is magnificent. The space and depth. The gradations of the sky. Magnificent. Nothing is missing that I can see. I . . . but I . . . need to look at it longer."

Despite my rapture, I realized it was critical to stop enthusing, and to get Van Nieuwpoort to tell me everything he knew about the painting. I felt instinctively that he was not involved in the business of the photographs. Someone else was pulling the strings.

I continued examining the painting while Van Nieuwpoort happily and ingenuously chatted on about his great-uncle's manor in the Ardennes, which he'd inherited, and about what a good fellow his great-uncle had been. What an enormous surprise it had been when one of his friends, Jane Caldwell — had I heard of her? he asked — had discovered the painting sitting in a corner of the attic when she came for a visit.

Jane Caldwell. I now understood the reason he had asked Caldwell to restore the work. The coincidence was more than intriguing.

"She's said to be quite . . . remarkable, this Jane Caldwell," I offered.

"Oh, yes, an exceptional woman," he replied.

His sad smile and the sidelong look were enough to

inform me that poor Van Nieuwpoort was the victim of unrequited love. He himself told me as much.

"I'm just a college chum to her, nothing more. She goes for looks. You know, beauty and that sort of business. Only thing that can touch her. Practically lives for it."

"She's not married, then?"

"Oh, no, no. Her standards are too high," replied Van Nieuwpoort. "Have to be someone out of a fairy tale for her. *And* look like her father."

We returned to the subject of Claude Lorrain, whom Van Nieuwpoort had become aware of only after Jane Caldwell told him the painting was authentic. Before then, Van Nieuwpoort might have seen Lorrain's works in the museum but not stopped to look closely at them.

And the *Libro di Verità*? A few weeks earlier it would have meant nothing to him. Finding out everything Van Nieuwpoort knew about his Lorrain was a simple task. Where art was concerned, he was artless.

The man's story was plausible; his sincerity was obvious. He was being manipulated, as I was. Somewhere there was an éminence grise, a shadow lurking behind the painting.

I told Van Nieuwpoort I needed a full week to examine the work in detail before giving a certificate of such historic importance. This seemed to pose no problem, and, after talking to Sotheby's officials by phone, he agreed to my request. Insurance matters would be arranged. I assured him my apartment had quite adequate security. Many of my own art works were very valuable, I explained, and they were carefully protected by alarm systems.

Someone from the auction house would come and pick the work up in precisely one week and take it to London, where any announcement of its "discovery" would await my confirmation.

As regards art experts, the general public is burdened with false impressions, due mostly to the tabloid press. Some feel these experts authenticate anything and everything so long as the thing has a signature — and so long as they can collect their fee. Others believe that art evaluators are bigoted and meanspirited souls who systematically refuse to authenticate any work that comes from some source other than their own gallery or museum.

There is some truth to both viewpoints. But when serious experts and auction houses are involved in a case, that is not how things happen. In France, whoever issues a certificate of authenticity is responsible for that certificate for a period of thirty years.

In the event that the work of art in question is the subject of debate or controversy, the expert needs to prove that the only way his expertise might be proved wrong is if some technique not available when he gave his certificate offers evidence for an alternate verdict.

There are plenty of exceptions to the rule that says it is nearly impossible and very rare that a painting — say, a work that has been discovered at a flea market — receives certification. The van Gogh museum in Amsterdam, normally very strict about such matters, had recently accepted the approval of a Swiss art expert regarding a still life signed by van Gogh and found at an antique fair. It was a fake. I had written a long, detailed article explaining why it was a fake, and how the expert in question had seriously compromised the whole business of art criticism by saying otherwise. The article, reprinted worldwide, received a good deal of attention, more than for any other article I'd ever written.

I would have loved then and there to have given my blessing to this painting. But its very perfection made me uneasy. Moreover, because of what had happened over the previous weeks, I could not look at this splendid piece of work with impartiality.

I walked around the painting, which sat in my living room on its easel, looking for flaws, seeking some tiny imperfection overlooked by everyone else. There had to be something wrong with this masterpiece. Why else would I have been put through such hell?

Could it be that by some strange irony all the engravings and lists Lorrain had so diligently assembled because of his fear of imitators might have aided and abetted the creation of a fake?

If it were a copy, it was a copy of genius. The painting breathed with life — it had a soul. I did not feel any sense of detachment. It was real. Yet someone had robbed me of the pure pleasure I should have felt. Joy had been poisoned.

Real or not, this painting was a trap. Whose? Was Van Nieuwpoort the work's sole proprietor?

I called my old friend Peter Mansfield at Sotheby's in New York. After much hesitation, and in strictest confidence, he informed me that the title holder of the Lorrain was an anonymous company headquartered in the Channel Islands. He gave me its name. Those islands (Dependencies of the British Crown, but governed by their own constitutions) are of course home to many offshore businesses whose owners wish to conceal their identities — and the source of their money. Getting access to their accounts was nearly impossible.

Peter told me he knew someone who had worked at the Treasury Department before starting his own information-gathering company. His services would cost me money, however. I told Peter I was willing to pay.

Two days later Peter called me back. Inquiries had been made. There were two principals in that company. Quentin Van Nieuwpoort was one. Jane Caldwell was the second.

Again Jane Caldwell. She had found the painting in the first place. She had restored it. She had authenticated it. Now she was joint owner. Caldwell was an expert on the restoration of seventeenth-century painting. She would know perfectly well that Charles Vermeille could not be taken in and was not for sale. She would also know that I would know if her painting were a forgery.

My nightmare had stemmed from flattery, flattery of my abilities and my integrity. What relief I felt was tempered by what I had been through.

Sometimes, in life, there come miraculous moments when you open your eyes to the morning light and the terrors of the night are banished. What do you do when nightmare and reality are locked as one? When there is no way of throwing off the cold hand of terror that grips you in sleep and in your waking hours? I thought of people driven mad trying to flee their terrors and who end up taking their lives.

I had been driven to the brink of madness, I knew that now. The only way to regain my sanity was to act.

A week later, the Lorrain painting was returned to Sotheby's, accompanied by my unequivocal certificate of authentication, declaring the work to be genuine. *The Port of Naples* would now make a rapid world tour — to Sotheby's branches in Paris, Geneva, Berlin, Sydney, Tokyo, and Los Angeles — before arriving in New York, where it would go on the auction block.

This tour posed some risks to the painting's safety. I suggested to Sotheby's that this masterpiece be sealed in an airtight glass-and-aluminum container, and immersed in a mixture of inert gases. A container of this sort had been used to preserve the mummy of Ramses II at the Louvre. One could still examine the work, but it would be out of harm's way. Once *The Port of Naples* arrived in New York, it could safely be removed from its protective shell.

I noted to Sotheby's that the Oxford Institute for Art Research was reputed to build these special boxes. Given that this extraordinarily valuable painting was on its way to London, why not leave the job to them?

Part II

Jane

7

Papa! I have done it! Oh, it is absolutely incredible. Was there ever such sweetness and light in the world? Not until now!

Papa, do forgive me. It's just that I am alive again. I've been *resurrected* — yes, that is the only word. Look at me. I've done this for you. For you! Look! I'm dancing with joy!

You've always hated it when I become emotional. Yet another sign that people with red hair are possessed. My red hair always did mortify you. Richard Caldwell and his scarlet daughter. You enjoyed telling me that in the Middle Ages women with red hair were burned alive. Yes, of course you were just being funny, just teasing. But you couldn't let it go, could you? All of my life you couldn't let it go. I think part of you believed I ought to have been burned.

It started when I was five. A tender age to be told you're a creature of the devil, wouldn't you say, Papa? That's the age when you most need love and reassurance. "My family has no red hair in it. I've really no idea where it came from." That was what you told people.

Well, Papa, it's still red. Like Titania, queen of the fairies. Like Elizabeth the First, who shook her red mane and dispatched the ships that defeated the mighty Spanish Armada. And what about Simonetta Caetano, Botticelli's Venus?

What you saw as a genetic flaw has become my glory, Papa. I'm in my glory! Watch me twirl! Do you remember when I was sixteen and you surprised me in my bath? I knew from your look that you were revolted that I had grown breasts. The horror! Your daughter had breasts! It was like Carlyle, or Ruskin, I forget which, discovering that his teenage bride had pubic hair. The idiot had thought she would be as smooth as a Greek statue. That was the only female nakedness he had ever seen.

I'm not afraid of death now. Really, I'm not. I have achieved what I most wanted. The masterpiece of my life is finished. And did you know that I'm in that masterpiece? Hiding in the corner, on bended knee, like a wealthy patroness.

Oh, how wonderfully bloody wonderful it feels to dance! Bare feet on moist grass. The grass here at the clinic is so green and lush. They really keep the grounds in wonderful condition. Something seems to be flowering at all times. Nature doesn't grieve. It blossoms, even in winter. Breathe in, Papa! The air is so pure.

How I would love to capture this landscape in paint — right here, right now. Hold its beauty. I could paint you, Papa, just the way I saw you a little earlier on the porch, sitting in your chair, your forearms posed on the armrests, your head inclined slightly forward. You looked like . . . like the Lincoln memorial. No less rigid, alas.

But I still hope for the miracle — that some glimmer of recognition will come to your eyes. A smile. Even a sigh. But there is nothing.

My God, what a nightmare your paralysis was in the beginning. I didn't think I could bear it. Now months and years have passed. I've accepted it. I will always keep hope, Papa, always. Sometimes when I hold your hand, I could swear you're squeezing mine, that something from the other side of the mirror is responding, some message from that world of silence in which your spirit has taken refuge.

I suppose I have always been waiting for recognition from something or someone. Something to justify my existence. I've always wished I had genius, to know that sudden, splendid understanding of immensity. To know inspiration bursting skyward like a geyser.

More than recognition. I have wanted to be declared "authentic." That's it exactly. "Jane Caldwell. Of Known Provenance." The phrase that appears on the fax here in my hand.

Genius? You never even believed I had talent. As far as you were concerned, it began and ended with my red hair. After Mother's death, the only warmth I ever found was in the company of my pony, grazing the gorse in Port Meadow. His moist muzzle offered more affection than your dry little pecks to my forehead.

"Say but one word, Lord, and your child shall be healed." I heard that phrase at church one day and it went straight to my heart. You see, if you had said just one word,

I would have been saved. A tiny gesture on your part to show you loved me. It would have been enough.

Instead I believed I needed to make you proud. I knew this would be hard work, and I worked hard. You know I did. I was determined to excel in something artistic — literature, or music, perhaps. I learned to play Chopin's études. I tried writing poetry. Do you remember? I memorized all of Keats's odes and most of Shakespeare's sonnets, as well. "Th' expense of spirit in a waste of shame."

In the end it was my first art teacher who offered me hope. My assignment had been to paint something freehand on an Oxford theme. I produced a watercolor of Lewis Carroll, whom I depicted waiting for Alice on an autumn evening on the Magdalen Bridge, where it crosses into the botanical garden.

A magical spot at a magical time of year. Autumns here in Oxford are unmatched in their beauty, don't you agree? "Season of mists," Keats has it. Mists seem to gather along the rooftops, making them fairylike. The whole city is washed, bathed in gray, gently illuminated by the sun.

It's our little paradise, isn't it Papa? Emerald lawns and ambling goats, students reading Herodotus under elms. Tame deer graze on lush grass turned golden by the sun's lengthening rays. Lines of dons in flowing gowns strolling along medieval walls. Young men in blazers and boaters punting with their sweethearts under weeping willows. The garden is full of dahlias. Leaves fly from cloister to cloister. Goldfish sparkle in the lake, near where the river runs through the meadow, with its wavy reflection of Magdalen Tower.

I was thinking of Turner when I did that watercolor. I

studied one of his paintings in a book and fell in love with his yellows. Ocher, liquid gold, and light browns — these were my delights.

My drawing teacher praised my work. Do you know I can still remember his words? "You have captured the air and light perfectly. This shows real talent, Miss Caldwell. You might paint one day."

How proudly I brought home my piece to show you. "Jane, you have a jaundiced eye." That was your reaction.

I should have been wounded by it but I wasn't. Oddly, you were paying me a compliment without knowing it. Turner also had a jaundiced eye, you see. That flaw was the basis of his genius.

So I kept painting landscapes bathed in their sickly yellow light. I got particularly good at doing cataclysms and catastrophes — world-engulfing and world-ending disasters: snow storms, avalanches, floods, hurricanes. I was taking all the frustrations trapped within me and spinning them into gold. Camouflaging them with bright light. They didn't go away, but the colors tinged them with melancholy and poignancy and gave them an aching sort of beauty.

You looked at my works and said it would be an abuse of language to call them "art." Someday, perhaps, you told me, I might get a job in the family business. But by then, Papa, your sarcasm was less devastating. I kept painting. It was all I had to save me when you sent me to that dreadful boarding school, at which, you said, I would receive the education my mother — God rest her soul — couldn't give me. You told the headmistress that I needed to be watched closely. I had a tendency to lie.

You were right. I did lie. I lied all the time. About my

feelings, my fears, my sadness. Unhappy children are always liars. They cannot tell true from false. Most true to me were my dreams of love. It was the world that was false.

The one place where truth and beauty remained was painting. I began to believe in my abilities, believe that they would bring me the joy for which I longed. Painting brought me serenity. I considered everything I saw from the perspective of shadows, lighting, and color combinations.

For all that, I didn't fall behind in my studies. I was always a good student. You know that, Papa. Once you even congratulated me. Do you remember? You said, "You've made a grammatical mistake on the last page of your essay on Chaucer." That meant that you'd read through the whole essay. This filled me with happiness. So you *were* interested in what I was doing! When I graduated at the top of my class, you said, "Perhaps you will make something of your life after all." From you that was dithyrambic praise indeed.

Then you had to ruin everything. Didn't you just. I wanted to attend an arts college and become a painter. Painting was my calling. I was responding to a power greater than myself. You wanted me to work in your chemical business, so that I could carry on your name — in the place of a stillborn brother, whose birth had killed the woman whose face I can only dimly remember, but for whom I grieve each day.

You had always taken care of everything, and your will was the ultimate authority in all matters. You and your ego were not to be denied. So when you informed me that I should become a biochemist, this wasn't a request, it was an order, a biblical command. Struggle was futile. I could have thrown myself at your feet and it would have made no difference.

What you never understood, Papa, was that a calling such as the one I felt, it was not something you can control and channel. Like a river it will always find its way to the sea, however it diminishes itself to get there, as a trickle, a stream, a creek. It will wait for its time and seek its outlet.

So I waited for my time. I pursued biochemistry at Oxford. Five dreary years studying nature's marvels through an electron microscope. But I made the best of it. I learned everything there was to learn about the physics of color, materials science, and the secrets of carbon 14 dating.

Even you could never have guessed how someday I would use this knowledge. Had you known, you might have preferred I'd enrolled in art school. By insisting that I become a biochemist, Papa, you gave me both weapons and an understanding of their use.

Be patient, Papa. Don't close your eyes. There's a point to all this. I'm trying to explain my actions, to show you the torturous path that led to this magnificent fake, this masterpiece I am now offering you on bended knee.

I'm going to implicate you. We're going to be partners in crime, you and I.

Do you know what I'm remembering just now? A bronze statue I once saw in the Père-Lachaise cemetery in Paris. It was of a recumbent man, holding in his hands the mask of a woman. She wore a sad smile and had large, lifeless eyes that stared at the man. He seemed to be trying to bring his mouth to hers. They are frozen within inches of each other. So near, yet light-years apart. Drops of rain fell from the yew trees and ran down the cheeks of the woman's mask like tears.

I used to fantasize that at night the statue came alive, that their faces could touch, that their mouths could whisper words of love to each other.

But I knew it wasn't true. Art is cold, like Keats's Grecian urn. The man would never console her, never kiss her tears away. One day, far in the future, the woman's head would crack and roll onto the moss and leaves and they would forever be separated.

And that is how far apart we are. Your pride made it that way. Your puritanical fear of women. I would guess that you made love with Mother with your eyes closed. There was no foreplay and no tenderness. You were depositing your seed.

You always thought I was an emotional wreck, but actually I've inherited some of your inability to express love. Oh, yes, of course, I have *fallen* in love. Quite often, actually — but only for long enough to be intrigued by the mystery of a man, and then to be disappointed. At first, sex was marvelous. After a lifetime of not being touched, being ravished was exquisite. Oh my, yes. But the moment of bliss would pass, and the men would feel like conquered terrain.

Boredom ended most of my affairs. Until I met Ambrose. He came to the company in response to an ad I had placed in the Oxford *Mail*. When he entered my office, I believed I perceived the outlines of happiness, happiness at last.

The one and only time I believed that perfection might have human form was when Ambrose looked at me. He reminded me of you, Papa. He had your profile, you see, your eyebrows, your deep voice. And he was a molecular biologist by training, just like you.

JANE

I have destructive tendencies. Those deep forces that drive me to demolish everything I construct. Ambrose was beautiful, but love was a hopeless wish. I had always emerged from it persuaded of the falseness of all feelings. Ambrose could have been everything I had always wanted. He was certainly everything you would have wished for me.

For that reason alone I knew we were doomed as a couple. Every time I looked at him a sixth sense tingled with premonitions of disaster. So I did absolutely everything wrong.

I hired him, knowing full well that I would jump into his arms the very next day even though office romances are silly, hopeless affairs. I spent my days seeking him out for no reason and then running away. I would drop by his lab on the spur of the moment, and watch impatiently for his return when he was having a meeting outside the office.

I loved him to distraction. And to extinction. Serenity in love was not my style. Love is not love when it becomes habit. Therefore I produced drama: I fretted and was jealous and suspicious. I turned our love into a tortured thing. When I didn't see him, I mentally dissected our previous meeting for hours on end.

The truth was Ambrose was too good-looking, too brilliant, too young, too loving, too too. I didn't deserve him and therefore I heaped my sins on him so that he would turn away. He did, eventually. He became afraid of someone so possessive and obsessive, particularly when working for her. He left seeking quieter pleasures.

Ambrose's departure, I felt, placed me squarely in the long line of tragic women: Dido, Phaedra, Medea. I wanted to die, you see, because I was predestined for unhappiness.

I nearly became anorexic, swallowing gallons of coffee, smoking three packs of cigarettes every day, working ridiculous hours. The paradox of all this self-destruction was that our family business started becoming very profitable.

Of course there were always people to console me. I would sometimes even forget I was a tragic heroine. I still found solace in a pretty face, in the abandonment an embrace can bring. I celebrated my despair with laughter, men, and spirits. I bought a Porsche and drove recklessly. I took up skydiving. Every day was a game of Russian roulette. Whee! The only way to live was in excess, with abandon.

Because I had been abandoned. By you. And by Ambrose.

Do you remember those letters I sent from boarding school declaring my love for you? I sent them by registered mail, so that you couldn't say you hadn't received them.

After your first stroke, I lived in the terror you would disappear altogether. You don't happen to recall what I said to you, do you? I said I didn't want to wait until you were on your deathbed before embracing you in the way that a daughter has the right to embrace her father.

You looked as if you had just gazed at Medusa. After I'd kissed you on the cheek, you said, "Your breath smells like garlic."

It was the cruelest thing you'd ever said to me. Cruel to the point of being hilarious.

Look at us now, Papa. For six years, you've been at my mercy. I can kiss you and hold you as much as I desire. I can tell you things that before would have made your flesh crawl. Perhaps you understand what I'm telling you. I do have the feeling my visits do you good. Perhaps even keep you alive.

The doctors smile when I tell them that. Contact of this sort, they reply, has no effect — but if it makes me feel better, then chat away by all means.

They tell me this with all the sympathy of an atheist talking to a mother praying at the tomb of her son.

The clinic's director doesn't share their skepticism, I'm glad to say. He's different. Before becoming director he worked at a hospital that specialized in the treatment of coma victims, and his experience with those patients has left him more cautious about making sweeping generalizations. Absence of reaction on a patient's part does not constitute absolute proof that he is oblivious to words and gestures.

I choose to believe him rather than the others. I want to believe that you can feel my hand on your cheek. I want to believe that you can still smell your favorite aftershave, which I brought you last week. I need to believe that you can hear me.

Don't sleep, Papa. Listen to me now, if only with your eyes. I'm getting to the crux of what I came to tell you. Everything I've said up to now is the truth. Now things get more complicated. What is false becomes inextricably mixed up in what is true.

8

Your second stroke left you completely paralyzed. The mighty oak had been felled. Never again would you wound me with sarcasm. Your active part in my life was at an end. I was delivered from your tyranny and the ice pick of your gaze. Your voice, which once had made me tremble, was silenced.

The first thing I did was sell your business. I had hated running it. I wanted to devote myself to Art, to satisfy the hunger gnawing deep inside of me, though I knew that by now the creative spark might have been extinguished.

I decided to open my own laboratory, specializing in the analysis and restoration of artwork. It seemed like the right place to begin.

Selling your business was complicated — and costly. After due diligence, and the government, lawyers, bankers, and accountants had taken their slices of the pie, I was left with enough money to place you in this clinic, and to equip my new lab.

Choosing the equipment was such fun. I was like a child in a toy shop. I wanted the most sophisticated gadgets money could buy: X-ray diffractometers, to study the crystalline structure of paint samples; electronic microscopes and ultrasound radiography, to analyze the physiochemical characteristics of materials; chromatographs that use a flame ionizer; an infrared reflectometer and spectroscope; macrophotographic machines.

I was fortunate enough to rent space next to a research laboratory with an ion accelerator and a nuclear ultrasound, replete with a measure chamber for detecting X rays, as well as a special lens system for magnetic focalization.

I know all this impresses you, Papa. You used to take such pride in keeping your business at the cutting edge.

My favorite machine of all was one I designed myself, by modifying an infrared X-ray spectrometer so that it could be put directly on an easel. This permitted me to perform experiments on the work, and make both qualitative and quantitative conclusions about the composition of the paint used by an artist. It holds the work in a vertical position, opposite a goniometer mounted onto a cart. That way I can minimize the size of the samples I need to take in order to study the pigments, strata by strata, on my microscope.

I also love the thing because it puts me in direct contact with the work of art. With a hypodermic needle I extract core samples, consisting of layers of superimposed materials. Naturally I am always very careful to identify the different control points where I've done this. The pinpricks are nearly invisible, even on an enlarged color reproduction of the work under examination.

Over time I compiled an enormous dossier, a veritable

data bank with samples from the paintings of all the great masters, as well as some by moderns whose works have been imitated, such as van Gogh, Matisse, Picasso, and Derain.

Really, Papa, it's rather impressive. I undertook an ambitious program combining visual and radiographic examination. The goal was to determine with precision the methods used by each artist in his painting. The macrophotographic apparatus and indirect light allowed me to read the painting's "handwriting," so to speak. I mean by that the way the paint takes to the canvas, the direction of the brush strokes, the distribution and density of the paint. In other words, all the techniques and motions that make up an artist's secret, and supposedly inimitable, signature.

I loved my work, Papa. I discovered every conceivable means of counterfeiting great artists, and I admired the sometimes prodigious gifts of certain forgers. Many of these copies were masterpieces in their own right.

The most spectacular fraud that I ever came across was an allegorical landscape being attributed to Poussin. It was done along the same lines as *Moses Saved from the Waters,* the painting that launched the age of heroic landscape.

The work was dense with symbols and imagery. The gentle waves of the Nile, which shimmers like a mirror, divide the space diagonally. On one riverbank are tombs, pyramids — the realm of ideas. On the other is the god of the river — the spiritual dimension. In the distance, an aqueduct — man's attempt to control nature. The boat symbolizes the voyage of souls.

I found that Poussin copy really quite moving. Whoever had imitated him had put a great deal of thought into it. He had known that Poussin was an artist of rare sophistication who had always studied his subject deeply before beginning work — which would happen only after he had mastered the visual language necessary to best express a particular scene.

All the tests I did on the painting's surface and on its pigments were favorable, but I'm afraid there were inconsistencies in the brush strokes and in the shading. Almost imperceptible, these inconsistencies, yet enough to reveal that the hand that had created this painting was not Poussin's.

After lengthy investigation, which I undertook personally, I succeeded in identifying the artist. He was Hungarian, and known for his nearly perfect imitations of contemporary and Impressionist works. He had made a mistake in trying to take on a classical painter.

I didn't turn him in, however. Do you know why, Papa? Because I thought that someday I might need his services.

Besides, at the time I was in a very forgiving mood. I was with Peter, the architect. He was incredibly handsome, more handsome even than you, Papa. I had met him at Oxford one magical evening, when I came across him sitting in the moonlight in the Port Meadows, playing Ravel's *Bolero* on his flute.

We came together like visions, soap bubbles, ephemera afloat on the wind. It was all so dreamlike.

Our love took place in a dimension that had nothing to do with our daily lives. Meeting was a way of fleeing reality, not embracing it, eschewing all those bothersome, bodily details — kisses that taste of nicotine, nakedness after lovemaking, flushing toilets. We wanted to live in allegorical time, not human time. We touched each other without touching.

You can't fornicate with an allegory. You don't put him in your bed, you place him on a pedestal.

This time I didn't abandon myself. And it was because I didn't abandon myself that Peter abandoned me. He went off in search of more fleshly happiness. Oh, how I hated him for this, Papa. Sometimes I wake up in the night with a thousand ideas for revenge spinning in my head.

Being abandoned by Peter sharpened my hunger for a world in which the idealized was possible. The world of art. I started spending all my free time at the National Gallery and in the British Museum. I even bought a flat off Russell Square so that when I was in London I could get to them easily.

I spent hours staring at paintings, and in particular those of Claude Gellée, known as "le Lorrain" and Claude Lorrain. He fascinated me most of all. I read everything I could about him. I wanted to know everything about his methods, his theories, his life.

And that was how I first heard about Charles Vermeille — through his remarkable studies of Lorrain. Vermeille did far more than teach me about Lorrain. He gave expression to my feelings about art itself. In his limpid, graceful prose I found thoughts I believed only I had — he seemed to have discovered the vocabulary for the miracle of creation. He was able to show how a work came to be.

I saw a photo of him in an art magazine and became infatuated. He was a bit old for me, and I knew perfectly well his appeal was as a father figure, but the look of penetration yet kindness was extremely seductive.

I wanted him to feel as I felt. Let it stand at that. I wanted him to look at me one day and recognize something.

Deep down, I knew that one day I was fated to meet this Charles Vermeille. You're probably laughing at me, Papa, but I need to tell you everything.

I often thought of writing him, telling him of my admiration. I must have started a dozen letters, then tore them up. Vermeille would have thought I was a lunatic.

The dream of meeting him did not become a reality until later. The occasion was a conference in Nice at which I was invited to speak. Oh, it was such an honor, Papa. Some of the world's greatest historians and curators would be attending. I took precious time away from work to prepare my talk.

Just thinking about that conference fills me with deep shame. But at the time, knowing that Vermeille would be there was exciting beyond words. I imagined all sorts of things — that he would fall in love with me, that he would see we shared a spiritual bond through Lorrain. Perhaps he would adopt me. My fantasies ran wild.

The gala dinner at the end of the convention. Oh my God. I remember doing myself up like a dream. I let my hair down. My turquoise lamé dress fit like a glove. A little eye shadow, a little rouge. I had never been so beautiful. When I crossed the filled dining room I could feel the collective gaze of the men.

Except for Vermeille, at whose table I'd been assigned. He looked at me coolly. There was no recognition. Out of politeness, he rose when I arrived at his table, bowed slightly when he took my hand, and pulled my chair out for me. Then he filled my wine glass, smiled, and went back to his conversation.

He clearly felt nothing. I was paralyzed with insecurity. Vermeille was sitting on my right. The man on my left was some squalid little art critic who kept breathing acrid breath down my neck. The room became a jangle of noise — the sounds of glasses and laughter and empty flattery. At our table attention revolved around Vermeille, this man with whom I was supposed to be sharing an intimate sense of connection. I sank immediately into a stupor. I felt mortally tired.

I had wanted to tell Vermeille how close I felt to him, but the words stuck in my throat. I drank glass after glass of wine to build up some courage, and when I did finally open my mouth I babbled like a schoolgirl. I wasn't eloquent, I was pathetic and simpery. To this day I haven't forgiven myself. I offered my heart to him on a platter, and he refused it.

Vermeille had looked at me without seeing me. He listened to me without hearing me. I was invisible to him, inconsequential. He didn't take my hand and say, "I've wanted to meet you for so long."

I barely remember running back to my room. The next morning I caught the first plane back to London.

A throbbing migraine haunted me for three days. It probably had something to do with the half bottle of Scotch I had drunk after this miserable spectacle, in an effort to forget the whole bloody thing. The pain was terrible, blinding me. I cried out every time I tried to move my eyes. I lost the sight in my right eye; the whole side of my face went numb. Oh, it was so frightening, Papa.

I ran to the bathroom to look at my reflection in the mirror, but nothing had changed. I looked the same. There was no disfigurement that I could see. I decided to call my doctor, but my legs would barely carry me to the phone. My hands had become cold and were tingling with pain. Dialing was agony.

The doctor told me not to panic but to come over straight away.

I have never been a hypochondriac. You know that, Papa. I am not the sort of person who scrutinizes every ailment and examines herself minutely all day long, complaining about every small ache and pain. But I will confess I was scared out of my wits when he made me move my eyes from right to left, and asked all sorts of questions that had nothing whatever to do with my eye. He wanted to know if I'd had any childhood diseases such as chicken pox, and at what age, and if I'd ever had difficulty walking, or felt any loss in sensation, or experienced involuntary muscle contractions.

What was so terrifying was that I had been feeling precisely these symptoms for some time. I had thought it was due to exhaustion. The doctor listened with careful attention, then replied that my vision would return in two or three days, but that I ought to make an appointment with an ophthalmologist.

I went immediately for the examination and returned to see my doctor that same afternoon with the results. He looked at them and started to drum his fingers.

"Fine, good. I don't think it's anything serious. My guess is that the optic nerve is in spasm. Probably a simple inflammation. Still, go to see a friend of mine at Radcliffe Hospital. It is important we learn the source of the inflammation."

I asked him if this was really necessary. He said it was. Best to tend to this immediately.

I went to Radcliffe Hospital. They kept me there for

three days, putting me through a battery of tests, each one more horrific than the other. There were MRI scans, spinal taps, blood tests, and reflex examinations. All this for a throbbing optic nerve? I wondered. My eyesight had returned, at least, as had the feeling in my face.

Finally they released me, having told me that the inflammation ought to go away by itself. I should live and work normally.

This was a good thing, for I had sunk all my money into my laboratory, and the default of the bank controlling your estate had nearly left you ruined. Oh, Papa. I was so worried I wouldn't be able to keep you at this clinic, and would have to transfer you to one of those dreadful state hospitals where the indigent and abandoned end up. How could I bear that? I needed to find some way to make money. Keeping you here costs five thousand pounds a month.

Before then I had somehow managed to equip the lab and cover the costs of this clinic. I eked out a living from my savings and from what I could get for my services. I knew that in the end the laboratory might go under and that I might have to liquidate everything.

We always had had an easy life, you and I. There was always enough for whatever we wanted to do. After your stroke, I took over your affairs. If there was any problem, I simply dipped into your accounts. They would be mine sooner or later, in any case. I never kept track of how much remained in them. You know perfectly well we never discussed money. That would have been vulgar.

That doesn't mean we shouldn't have talked about it. Or found some way of accumulating more of it. A great deal more. With a heavy heart I sold two small Reynolds I had bought when I was running the company and felt flush. The proceeds meant you could stay in the clinic for another six months. I prayed that would tide us over until I could find a way of replenishing the family coffers.

I knew I would do anything I could to become rich.

9

I had never borrowed money from anyone. I'd never had to. But it seemed quite natural that the first person I would think of should be Quentin Van Nieuwpoort. Quentin had been mooning after me since we were at Oxford together. Asking him for help would be a delicate matter, given his feelings for me, but he was, after all, an old friend. A wealthy admirer.

So I thought of him while pacing around my storeroom among all the frames, easels, rolls of that special tissue used to repair damaged canvasses, and cases of dissolvents.

My eye caught a ruined old wreck of a painting I'd bought from Quentin a few years before.

It was shortly after he'd come into an inheritance from a great-uncle who died just short of his one hundredth year and left Quentin a country estate in the Ardennes. Shortly after his great-uncle's funeral, Quentin invited me to come visit. I accepted the invitation. It was October, and I knew how beautiful the Ardennes would be.

Quentin's estate was situated deep in the forest. It was a kind of Gothic folly, built during the medieval revival in the midnineteenth century with turrets and crenellated walls and leaded windows. A man's castle, that sort of thing — though it had undeniable charm and a stunning view.

We spent the afternoon nosing around the place and looking in forgotten corners. There were not more than fifteen rooms, each one crammed with dusty and rather hideous hunting trophies.

After a picnic lunch in the dining room, whose ceiling, not unattractively, was painted after the Italian fashion, we decided to have a look round the attic. I have always adored attics. Every dusty trunk or hat box might contain some treasure.

We found trunks of dresses with Belgian lace and corsets, porcelain vases, boxes of letters, pictures without frames, frames without pictures. In a corner under a canvas stiff with age was a very old-looking framed painting. It had been long neglected, but we could just make out the dim outlines of a landscape, the tops of a few trees, and, in the left-hand corner, painted prettily though covered with grime, some classical ruins.

I dabbed at the painting with a handkerchief to see what was hiding beneath the dust.

"Who knows," I said to Quentin. "It may be worth something."

We brought the painting closer to a window and I examined it from all angles. All I could make out was a confusion of indistinct and damaged images, spotted with mold. Time and humidity had taken their destructive toll on the poor old thing. The painting was a shambles. Still, the frame and supports were in reasonably good shape, and the canvas didn't seem to have been too damaged.

"Looks like a total loss, I'm afraid," said Quentin. "I'll have it carted out to the rubbish."

One should never say such a thing to a restorer. My new career involved bringing "unreadable" paintings back to life.

"Quentin, I'll tell you what. I'll buy the painting from you for a hundred pounds. Have it sent to Oxford. If I manage to restore it, and if it turns out to be worth something, we'll split the proceeds fifty-fifty. Sound all right?"

Quentin of course wanted to give me the painting outright, but I insisted. In the end he gave in with a grin.

My initial bravado behind me, I put the painting in my Oxford storehouse and in the back of my mind, telling myself that one day I'd have a crack at it.

Anyway, as I say, I was pacing around the storeroom when it caught my eye. This was the time to have a look at the thing, I suddenly thought. I took it to the lab, rolled up my sleeves, and went to work. Two precious days I spent trying to salvage that wreck, only to discover in the end that it was a pleasant and innocuous landscape of absolutely no distinction. A few cattle grazing among Roman ruins. It had doubtless been painted in the seventeenth century by some Italian hack. Most certainly no masterpiece.

I might have gotten three hundred pounds for the painting, but I decided to keep it. I liked the frame, which was original. And, God knows why, I thought it might one day prove useful.

Meanwhile, I continued to look for ways to make money. I needed it for you, for me, and to pay off my debts. I spent money I didn't have to place advertisements for my laboratory in art magazines, in the hope of attracting the notice of European curators.

And I continued to marvel at the works of Lorrain wherever I traveled. *Temple in Delphi* in Rome; the religious works in the Prado; *Hagar, Ishmael, and the Angel* at the Pinakothek in Munich; *Dido and Aeneas* in Hamburg; and the extraordinary *Psyche Saved From the Water* at the museum in Cologne.

The more of his work I saw, the more I seemed to discover things about myself.

Yes, Papa, I know. Some might find this passion for Lorrain just a little strange. Most people might not even stop to look at his paintings when passing by them in a museum.

Understanding his work takes time. His is a world of visual poetry and subtle harmony. One needs to find a way to respond to him.

Lorrain's universe is not for everyone. His work provides a refuge, a place of dreams, of airy landscapes and inner peace. The whole point is not just to look at what he is showing you, but to experience it. The gentle breeze wafting through those magnificent valleys and refulgent landscapes. The sun descending behind trees and mountains. The smell of roses at that magic moment when dawn dissolves to day. Lorrain gives us visions of paradise lost, and one's reaction can only be that of deep longing. What are those lines of poetry, I forget whose?

> To hear the lark begin his flight
> And, singing, startle the dull night,
> From his watch-tower in the skies
> Till the dappled dawn doth rise;

* * *

The strange pains I'd experienced earlier came back while I was returning from a trip to Rome. Tingling in the fingers, painful inflammation in the legs, terrible migraines.

"Not to worry," my doctor told me over the phone. "You're tired and you're under stress. It's nothing."

I waited for the symptoms to go away, but after a week they didn't. I went to see the doctor and again he sent me to the hospital for yet more tests.

Do you know that pain that seizes your entrails and makes you think the world is coming to an end? For five days in hospital I lived face to face with this dreadful reality. After the second exam — a myelograph test, I think — I knew what the doctors were looking for. Their elliptical comments made it all the more clear: the shaking, the migraines, the ataxia, the paresthesia. It all amounted to one thing: multiple sclerosis.

I felt condemned, Papa, condemned to a death that would come in small installments. Each crisis would get worse. I've seen someone die that way before. It is the way you are dying. And while waiting for it I would live in terror of the next attack. What would be the first to go? My eyes? My mind? Would I have to be restrained? The interval between the two first crises had been short. The disease would now progress rapidly.

I would die unsatisfied, unfinished. The imminence of death posed unbearable questions: Why had I been born? What had I done with my life? I had spent my life waiting. "I wasted time and now time doth waste me."

On the fifth day of my stay in the hospital, my doctor came into my room and sat on my bed. He was smiling.

"Miss Caldwell, you've got an hour to pack your bags

and leave. After midday, checkouts are postponed to the next day."

"What do you mean?" I asked.

"What I mean is that there is absolutely nothing whatever the matter with you."

He explained that the symptoms had been caused by a virus that went undetected the first time around, and whose symptoms are exactly the same as for multiple sclerosis.

The first thing I did when I got out of the hospital was run to see you to tell you the joyful news. I half expected my release would bring about your own.

We shared a glass of champagne. Don't you remember, Papa? I sat with you until late into the evening, near the window, watching night fall over the trees in the park.

In my euphoria — my tipsiness, I suppose — I felt as if something had happened between us. Something, well, like the breath of life, life that would continue to be mine for a little longer. Perhaps you felt something.

Then my joy seemed to collapse under the weight of the certainty that it was too late for you and me. Always, forever, too late. You were somewhere else now. You always had been. Light-years from me.

I left you, Papa, to go and taste something more of life. I wanted to make life. I went to the house of a former lover and simply gave myself to him. I didn't have to say anything. We rolled together in a voluptuous union that had the urgency of death. Time's wingèd chariot.

The next morning I faced once again our financial problems. I, Jane Caldwell, thirty-eight years old, beautiful, gifted, filled with regrets about her life yet driven by a crazy desire to do something grand, something wonderful, something that would turn her life around.

I would create an immortal work of art before death, which had brushed against me once, made a second pass.

A revelation came to me during one of my meditative visits to the National Gallery.

I was sitting on a bench in the little rotunda that houses the Turner painting, the one the artist himself had bequeathed to the museum — with the stipulation that it be surrounded by two Lorrain paintings that he had also donated. As usual, I was lost in reverie before these luminous portals, but this time my feelings of immersion were tempered.

I realized that I knew every brush stroke as if I had done them myself. I knew why he had put such and such an architectural caprice there, what diagonal he had used to give the effect of the horizon, what mixture of colors he had used to get that yellow.

Never would I create something as sublime. I had knowledge; I lacked genius. I needed to accept that mine was a modest talent.

"Modest talent." The words did not accord well with my passionate temperament. Something was pushing me into believing I could find a way.

Suddenly my whole body was flooded with a sense of relief, with the conviction that leaves no room for doubt: I would create a Lorrain. The artist himself would guide me.

I knew I had found my destiny, Papa. I also knew exactly how the thing could be done. It was a flash of genius — a total vision.

The minute I got home to Oxford I ran to my lab and found the painting I'd bought from Quentin.

The first thing I needed to do was remove all traces of the original paint from the canvas — but preserve the varnish deposited there over the course of the centuries. Using a mild solvent, I removed these layers one by one. I would reuse the varnish later, because the dust embedded in it was authentic, and therefore would confirm the finished painting's age.

Whenever I could — weekends, holidays — I locked myself away in my laboratory to analyze, decompose, and then reconstitute all the pigments necessary.

I had already compiled a complete list of the paints Lorrain used, as well as details of their chemical composition. I knew, for example, that the blues in his oceans consisted of fine particles of lapis lazuli dissolved in white lead. I couldn't use just any lapis, at least not the sort you find on the open market, which comes from Brazil or Africa. I needed old lapis, extracted from the legendary mines near the mouth of the Amu Darya River in Tajikistan. The crystal composition is unique.

For the blue of the sky, I would need azurite, a copper deposit you can find on fragments of bronze Roman statuary, mixed with equal amounts of palm pulp.

Lorrain's vermilion consisted of mercury sulfide. The green, copper oxidized in a natural resin. The yellow was not natural ocher, but a massicot, a lead-tin oxide.

In one week, using an X-ray spectrometer, I had reconstituted the entire color palette Lorrain had used during his Italian period. This palette did not include, for example, the English vermilion, which he didn't adopt until the end of his life.

The quality and origins of the fur Lorrain used in his brushes was the subject of further painstaking research, because a few hairs always remain behind, lodged in the painting. The presence of any modern element in the finished work would give the whole thing away.

I took all my materials to my flat in London, where I had the basic equipment I needed.

By then I had decided my painting would be Lorrain's missing masterpiece, *The Port of Naples*. It had disappeared sometime in the nineteenth century, but there are various engravings and copies that give us a very good idea of what it must have been like. The original drawing could of course be found in the *Libro di Veritá*. All I needed to do was increase the scale of that drawing and come up with a precise schematic.

I carefully removed the painted canvas from its frame, taking care to put each hand-wrought iron tack back into its original hole. Then I secured the canvas to my worktable.

The next step involved removing the pictorial layers, abrading them by hand until I hit canvas. Using solvents on the varnish-free paint would have meant running the risk of leaving a mark on the back of the canvas.

Over the years, I had categorized the various fabrics Lorrain used while in Italy. His preference was for what is termed *armure toile,* a simple canvas of threads, woven in pairs or singly, forming a weave with a density of ten to thirteen threads per square centimeter. The disposition of the threads and the weave were common at the time in France and Italy. Luck was with me. The density of the weave and the direction of the width of the painting from Quentin's attic painting corresponded perfectly.

The tightly woven linen canvas retained a part of its original preparation, though no further trace of the original landscape. I double-checked that every trace of it was gone. The last thing I needed was to have a "ghost" image of the original appear while the finished painting was being examined.

Using broad strokes, I applied a supplementary base of red ocher, fabricated according to a formula employed by many painters in the seventeenth century: a combination of ferruginous clay, rich in silicates and relatively poor in oxides, and linseed oil.

Once this thick layer of colored ocher was dried, I spread a thin transitional layer, made up of equal parts of clay and lead oxide, plus carbon I obtained from burning antique wood. The composition of this layer was one of Lorrain's trade secrets. It rendered the colors in his finished paintings even more luminescent.

You must understand, Papa, that these primary coats, these intermediaries between the canvas and the pictorial elements, were of critical importance for the survival of a painting over the course of centuries. That is why the masters attended to them with such care.

Funny, isn't it? If you hadn't forced me to study biochemistry, I never would have been able to accomplish any of this. Then again, had I gone to art school and become a painter, I doubt I would have even imagined imitating a seventeenth-century painter — though I might have mastered some of the techniques necessary. This Lorrain came to be at the end of a tortuous path, Papa. A path you set me on.

I knew that for the actual painting I needed an actual

painter, not a dreamer and a dabbler like me. I needed a forger of real genius.

I chose the man who had painted that Poussin I had uncovered several years earlier, the one I told you about. I had been right in thinking that one day I might have need of his services. That day had come.

His name was Imre Dagy. He was a compatriot of the Hungarian counterfeiter Elmy Hoffmann of Hory, and had taken refuge in London after the failed 1956 uprising in Hungary. Dagy earned a living by giving painting lessons. His talent was undeniable, but his linguistic and commercial skills were not at the same level, and he soon found himself involved with a network of art forgers in the employ of a disreputable London dealer, a sort of Fagin of the art world.

Dagy's ill health and his phobia of the world had kept him from reaching the attention of the public. For my purposes, this was ideal.

Finding him took time, but find him I did. He was living in a studio off Portobello Road. To reach his studio you went through a courtyard where a dealer stored his goods, and down a long, dark hallway, until you came to a steep set of stairs, covered in grime, leading to his attic. It was like something out of Dickens, I swear. The whole place reeked of dust and decrepitude.

I knocked. The door opened a crack. Then the artist himself appeared, his face barely visible by the hall light.

"You are looking for someone?" he asked with a thick accent, but with a gentle smile. I don't think he had many visitors.

He was not a handsome specimen, this Hungarian. His nose was elongated at the bottom, his forehead sloped, and he had long, stringy gray hair. His eyes were half closed under heavy lids. And he had a way of not looking straight at you.

Yet his hands were rather beautiful, though marred by liver spots and paint.

He invited me into his hovel. Among the dusty bric-a-brac my eye kept on returning to the torso of a woman in plaster, her eyes looking ecstatic and her breasts extended. Such vulgarity. There were figurines in painted plaster — the sort you see in souvenir stalls.

"Do you like these statues? I am the sculptor of them."

I thought I must have the wrong address. This man could not possibly have created that wonderful Poussin. He seemed incapable of creating anything of beauty.

Next to catch my eye was a hideous creation depicting naked women standing on plinths in front of a grove of trees; others were hidden in the folds of theater curtains. Truly ghastly.

"I am a specialist of the trompe l'oeil," he said, a note of pride in his voice.

How was I to reply to that? They were staggeringly ugly.

Yet something intrigued me about him. He seemed so — I don't know — empty. Like a hollow husk of a man.

I stayed for a few hours in his home, listening to him talk, trying not to look at the eyesores around me. Like many lonely people, he talked when given half the chance. The details he provided of his life left an indistinct picture. Something about it lacked life.

His father had been a sculptor who in the '30s had been awarded a Rome Prize, and had taken advantage of it to abandon his wife and son and move to Italy with his model.

The poor wife did her best to raise her son by herself, and sent him to school in Budapest.

Young Imre was talented at many things, but his youth in Communist Hungary consisted of a series of failures. He'd never been able to find his place, though he considered the Soviet regime's inability to recognize his gifts as proof of his genius.

Having been *almost* a medal winner in painting at the School of Fine Arts in Budapest, he failed to get a degree in architecture. That didn't stop him from drawing up plans for the new parliament, though the name that went on the plans was that of some incompetent apparatchik. He had left his country in the chaos that followed the 1956 uprising. His mother had died by then, and there was no reason to remain behind.

He came to London, where as I said he eventually turned to doing forgeries.

As he grew older, he dreamed more and more of the day when the world would recognize his gifts, when he could return to a Budapest liberated from the Communist yoke. There, life was cheap. For several thousand pounds a year you could live like Prince Esterházy.

When Dagy seemed to have finished recounting the pathetic story of his life, I asked him about the Poussin copy I'd discovered some years earlier. Had he indeed been the painter of that flawed but magnificent piece of work?

He regarded me suspiciously, offering no reply. Then a glimmer of pride and pleasure came into his eyes. He could tell I had not asked him this in order to report him to the authorities.

"Yes, miss. That was my painting."

Without revealing to him that I had been the one to discover it was a fake, I made him my proposition: hiring him for some confidential work for which he would be handsomely compensated. I named a sum. He looked at me as if I were the angel of the Annunciation. We had a deal.

That same evening, having paid off his room and his debts with some money I gave him, Dagy moved into the guest room of my London flat. I had turned it into a studio, thinking that one day I might use it to paint. It was large, and very bright, and had a pretty view of an inner courtyard with a garden. Dagy was like a man transformed. He began to take on life.

10

This was a magical period in my life. I felt keenly alive to the truths to be found in Lorrain's work by participating in the creation of a fake. Rather paradoxical, don't you think, Papa? Imre threw himself into our adventure with enormous passion. We engaged in deep and protracted analyses of Lorrain's work. We pored over reproductions of his paintings. As often as we could we went to museums to look at Lorrain's paintings in the flesh, and spent hours studying them.

Most of all, we studied the copies of *The Port of Naples* as if our very lives depended upon memorizing every detail. How wonderfully ironic that the *Libro di Veritá*, poor Lorrain's hedge against imitations, was proving so useful a tool for creating a copy.

It was rather romantic, actually. Imre and I were living through Lorrain. Everything we saw was filtered by his eye, his vision. When we walked through Hyde Park we would discuss how Claude — as we began to refer to Lorrain familiarly — might have painted it. We dreamed of Arcadian worlds. Most of all, we tried to express what it is about Lorrain's use of light that gave his paintings such life. How did he create those reflections? How did he manage to capture the gradual intensification of daylight and then dissipate it into mists?

After a month of talk and research, Imre sat down and began work. After a second month of intensive work, he had completed the initial sketch. Watching him was mesmerizing. He composed with astounding assurance, without hesitation or second-guessing. At times I felt I was watching Lorrain himself at work. Imre was possessed. There is no other word for it.

Toward the end, he began using his beautiful hands to blend the colors. Lorrain often did this, you see. Luckily none of the prints were clean enough for positive identification.

Then it was finished. He signed it "Claudio G.I.V. 1636 Napoli."

The inner fire that Imre had brought to his work was extinguished the moment he set down his brushes. He had exhausted himself. He looked as he had when I first met him at his hovel off Portobello Road. He counted his money and slipped it into an inside pocket of his coat. When we said our farewells, however, a glimmer of triumph shone in his eyes.

"Thanks to you I have done my masterpiece. Now I can die in peace."

He used the money to return to Budapest. He died of cancer soon afterward.

I am sorry for this. Imre would have rejoiced at the news that his life's achievement had been authenticated.

My real work began after his departure. First I threw myself into studying how paintings age, so that I could reproduce the sort of very fine craquelures and fissures that appear over time. The uneven pace with which the layers dry — much depends on the binders and individual colors involved — makes aging a complex process. Add to that the scars that result from the stretching caused by the wood frame, as well as the scratches and scrapes that happen to all paintings as soon as they leave the artist's studio.

Few paintings escape the ravages of time. There are some pristine examples, such as those belonging to the British royal family. But most works of art have been affected by wars, fires, and changing ownership. The percentage of sixteenth- and seventeenth-century paintings that have survived intact is actually quite small.

I had studied and evaluated most of the means by which forgers try to accelerate the aging process. Methods that had worked in times past, even as recently as a generation ago, no longer sufficed, given new technology. I was therefore forced to seek new ones. Of particular help were articles written by museum curators, who readily disclosed all their findings and conclusions as a way of proving their meticulous superiority in such matters — and the indisputable authenticity of the works in their collections.

For example, I learned that the age and composition of dust trapped in the paint often give fakes away. Therefore I was careful to use venerable dust, carefully harvested from beams in old churches.

The cracks gave me the most difficulties. I applied coats of varnish, composed of the resins I had taken from the original painting, to create the right network of craquelures, which, in any old painting, are never perfectly superimposed.

At long last the painting was finished. I checked and double-checked my work until I was convinced I had done everything humanly possible.

I provided the first certificate of authenticity for *The Port of Naples*. After all, I had appointed myself the official restorer of Quentin's painting. I declared that this was indeed a genuine Claude Lorrain. My opinion would carry some weight, of course, though I knew it would not be definitive.

Oh, but Papa, with what maternal anxiety did I send the painting off to Los Angeles for its second appraisal. The whole time it was gone I was biting my nails. There was always the possibility, the distinct possibility, that I had overlooked some detail. I imagined the work under ultraviolet light, being bombarded with X rays and gamma rays. I saw men in white lab coats with magnifying lenses scrutinizing every square inch of the surface. Then there would be the spectrometer test, and after at that, chemical analyses.

I tried to stay calm, reminding myself that even the most brilliant experts using the most advanced equipment can make mistakes. Five French experts had authenticated a phony van Gogh. Abraham Bredius, the famous Dutch specialist, had declared that a Vermeer copy painted by Van Meegeren was "certainly one of Vermeer's finest works."

Then I panicked again, remembering that ten years after the Van Meegeren episode, a relatively obscure restorer noted that the painting contained an anachronism and was therefore most certainly a fraud. In the work was a jar with two handles — of a sort not available in Vermeer's day.

In my Lorrain were all sorts of objects that might shout anachronism to someone knowing what to look for. Those masts and loading docks. The drawing in the *Libro di Verità* hadn't provided every detail. Had we gotten them right?

But the Griffith supported my claim, Papa. They said I had found a true Claude Lorrain, and none other than *The Port of Naples,* listed as painting number six in the *Libro di Verità*. The work had gone missing sometime in the nineteenth century.

Soon the world will have the news. Art experts and critics will bow their heads. "Genius!" they will say when they look at this forgery.

Sotheby's has agreed to manage the sale. I insisted it be done in New York. Can you imagine? The whole room will quiver with amazement when the painting is carried in. Thunderous applause will follow the final tap of the ivory hammer.

We will be rich, Papa. I'm told the painting will bring millions.

There was one last hurdle. Sotheby's requested the work be submitted to Charles Vermeille for a final, and decisive, evaluation.

I was afraid this would happen. I had also expected it. If Vermeille decided the work was a forgery, all would have been lost.

Vermeille's involvement, inevitable though it perhaps was, put everything at risk. I couldn't allow that. Thinking about it kept me awake nights. What could I do? Not permit the work to be submitted for his evaluation? Not possible. Make him disappear? I knew he was in good health. I'd learned a great deal about him since I began working on my Lorrain. I knew his life, his habits, his rituals. I knew all about his legendary integrity.

Damn him and his integrity! I found his writing on the subject of forgeries high-handed and self-serving — he had written for example a very long article about that expert who pronounced the van Gogh work authentic. Not only had the poor man betrayed his country and his honor, in Vermeille's eyes, he had betrayed history itself. The job of the art critic was sacred. Such sanctimoniousness.

It was while reading that article that I began thinking of ways to make him compromise his unflinching probity. This would not be easy. Vermeille was an immensely proud man, as I had discovered in Nice. He held himself to a different standard.

There was something. Not a flaw, but a vulnerability, I discovered. He adored his son, his only child.

We would see just how dear his honor was to him when compared to the thing he most valued in the world.

How would I make him afraid for his son? It was really very simple. Nothing is more terrifying than an invisible enemy, a threat that will not declare itself. I didn't want Vermeille to panic. I needed to unnerve him gradually and inexorably, like a Chinese torture that, drop by drop, would drain his spirit.

I decided to send him photos of his son. Anonymously. Mailed from all over the map.

I saw them together once when I was in Paris. They were coming out of an apartment building. Vermeille was laughing at something Jean-Louis had said. They looked as if they were enjoying themselves. It almost made me ashamed of what I would do.

I learned that Jean-Louis Vermeille was planning to continue his studies in California. A month later I went to Berkeley. I dyed my hair black, then pulled it back into a chignon and put on large horn-rimmed glasses. I decided to pretend I taught at a British university and was visiting Berkeley to give a talk on genetic botany.

I had taken with me a small but very sophisticated little camera, with a built-in telephoto lens. Locating my prey was not difficult. I found him playing tennis — he was extraordinarily good, of course, good enough to attract attention from spectators. You could see how hard he concentrated on his game. Quietly taking a picture without anyone seeing me was child's play.

A couple of days later I took a second photo of him eating lunch on the lawn with some friends. Jean-Louis's routine was incredibly active. In addition to playing tennis, he surfed and jogged. I managed to photograph him doing both. I had fun with the jogging photo, which I took with my telephoto lens from behind a tree in Charles Lee Tilden Park, on the edge of campus. The area bore an uncanny resemblance to a Lorrain landscape, with its large trees, shrubs, the sun filtering through the leaves, the magical glow of twilight. All I needed was a classical ruin or a figure from myth dancing in the corner.

Later when the photo was developed, I noticed that something — the reflection of the sun off the lens, perhaps — had made a small red dot on Jean-Louis's forehead. It looked like it had been caused by a laser sight. I was certain Vermeille would think a gun had been trained between the eyes of his beloved son. It would heighten his anguish. So much the better.

The day after that I actually met Jean-Louis. I knew this was unwise. What if later he were to see a picture of me in some professional magazine while visiting his father? Was my disguise good enough? Still, I couldn't resist. He was sitting in the cafeteria where I took my meals. The seat in front of him was vacant, so I sat down and smiled. He smiled back. When I'd finished my milkshake I took out a map of the campus and pretended to look for something.

"Such a large campus," I said, sighing. "I'm a little lost. I'm sorry to bother you, but would you have any idea where the botanical library might be located?"

"No, I have no idea. But here, let me have a look at your map."

We both studied the map. He explained that he himself had recently arrived on campus and didn't yet quite know his way around. We talked about other things — my field, his studies, surfing, the beauty of Northern California.

I liked him immediately. He was young but very charming. And incredibly handsome. I wished I were ten years younger, so that I could let down my hair and flirt openly, rather than get to know him by subterfuge. I wanted to please him, like an eighteen-year-old — without artifice.

In any case, I seemed to have succeeded in attracting him, for the next thing I knew he was proposing to give me a tour the following day, which was Saturday, so that I wouldn't leave Berkeley without first admiring its many beauties. Then he accompanied me all the way to the botanical library, and told me where he lived.

Later I waited outside his building for a few hours. He came out on his balcony. I took another photo.

The last photo I took on the little dock where Jean-Louis took me for a walk before dinner at a North Beach bistro. It was around eight in the evening. The light from the setting sun gave everything a golden hue, eerily like the colors in *The Port of Naples*. The depth of the horizon, the slightly choppy waters, the port itself. Then Jean-Louis walked right up to the water's edge and stood for a moment on the loading dock and gazed at a boat in the distance. Again, he didn't see me take the picture.

I imagined what Vermeille would think when he saw it. I knew he would notice the parallels between the photo and the Lorrain painting. An amateur would have seen them.

I must say, Papa, that I spent a wonderful evening with Jean-Louis. Oh my! I would have loved to have stayed in Berkeley for longer. I probably would have slept with him. But I needed to get back home to set in motion my little plan.

The first thing to do was send Vermeille the photos, one by one. I decided upon the order, leaving the Lorrainesque photos for last, of course. The rest was easy. I was doing a fair amount of traveling at the time and I simply dropped them in the mail wherever I happened to be.

At first, I was amused by the idea of Vermeille looking at these photos, his brows furrowed, pacing nervously in his study, trying to think of who could possibly be responsible for them. I knew for certain that he would phone Jean-Louis and ask him who had taken it. Then he would have put it up somewhere, kept it in sight. He was vain about his son. With good reason.

His worries would really begin with the second photo. Vermeille was the sort of father who fretted. Suspicions would start to preoccupy him, keeping him from concentrating on his own work. He would dread going down to fetch his mail every morning.

The third photo would come as a shock, a very rude shock. Though I am childless, I could imagine the pain. Interesting, isn't it? It was precisely because I am childless that I could put Vermeille into such pain. I often wondered, Papa, how you would have felt had this happened to you. I'm afraid to know the answer.

Vermeille wouldn't have any idea what to make of the photographs. They would not just preoccupy him, they would obsess him. He would feel powerless. What can you do about an invisible threat? Impotence and rage would grow with every passing day. I could picture him, waiting for the phone to ring.

The fourth photo would turn him into a caged animal. The press clipping I'd included about the death of Onassis's son would terrify him. He would be prepared to sell his soul to save his son.

The clipping was gratuitous, I realize that. But I couldn't help it. I wanted this man on his knees. He would pay for having ignored me. His exalted integrity would turn to ash.

Keep your eyes open a little longer, Papa. I'm not finished with my confession.

How I made that poor man suffer! And yet, in the final analysis, it was because I admired him so much. I tried so hard to justify what I was doing. I told myself he was guilty. Guilty, first of all, of resembling you. Guilty of loving his son like a mother would. Guilty for being so sure he knew the truth. Guilty because he was about to prove himself a hypocrite and authenticate a fake.

The fifth photo, of Jean-Louis jogging, would begin to open his eyes. The Lorrainesque look of the landscape might have been an accident, a coincidence, but it very easily could have been intended. Something would happen in his mind. The penny would drop. He would believe he had seen the photograph before.

This part of the game I rather enjoyed. It added a touch of class to what was really a fairly unpleasant business.

The whole time this was happening I watched my reflection in the mirror, looking for changes. I expected to see an evil leer, a malicious glint. If anything, I seemed to have become more beautiful. My eyes were clearer and brighter.

The sixth photo, of the port of San Francisco, Quentin's phone call, and hearing about the painting would dispel any lingering doubt in Vermeille's mind. He would believe his son's life depended upon his issuing a certificate of authenticity.

He has. So, I've won, Papa. The news is here in my hand. The money will mean that we can spend happy days together, you and I, here in this beautiful clinic. I will be more at peace with myself.

Perhaps I will begin to paint again.

Final Touches

On a chilly December evening, a day before a major auction was to be held at Sotheby's in New York, Charles Vermeille landed at Kennedy Airport. He had taken the Concorde as a special treat.

After getting through customs, he took a taxi to the Carlyle. He always stayed there, enjoying the calm and elegance of this Manhattan institution. It was perfectly located for visits to the Metropolitan Museum and was a fairly easy walk to Sotheby's as well.

He got up early the next morning feeling physically refreshed — the Concorde had dramatically reduced jet lag, of course — and decided to walk down to Sotheby's. The sky was like lapis lazuli, and New York, particularly on a splendid morning such as this, was pure pleasure to him.

When he entered the enormous concrete and glass structure that was the new Sotheby's, Vermeille noted that the uniformed guard scrutinized him carefully. He realized that he must appear anxious, lacking his usual self-possession. He decided he needed to take a few minutes to compose himself before confronting his colleagues from the art world, so he went down to the lower gallery.

On display were posters announcing upcoming sales at Sotheby's auction houses around the world. And, to commemorate its most glorious moments, Sotheby's had done beautiful reproductions of van Gogh's *Irises* and *Doctor Gachet,* Picasso's portrait of Fernandez de Soto and his *Les Noces de Pierrette,* as well as Renoir's *Au Moulin de la Galette,* the originals of which had commanded record prices at auction.

Vermeille sipped an espresso he picked up at the little cafeteria. After a moment, he felt more in command of himself, and headed back to the wide granite staircase leading to the second floor.

He was halfway up when a voice stopped him.

"Hello, Charles!"

Vermeille turned to see Egon Adalbert, who promptly grabbed his hand and began pumping it. He hadn't seen Adalbert in weeks, and, since he had been one of the people Vermeille had first suspected about the photographs, he was at a loss for words.

"I was certain you would be here. Not every day that a Lorrain goes up for sale, is it my friend? Particularly one that you yourself have authenticated."

Adalbert was brandishing a Sotheby's catalog on whose cover was, in glorious full color, *The Port of Naples.*

Vermeille managed to say, somewhat unenthusiastically, what a pleasant surprise it was to see his old colleague before Adalbert launched into a discussion of the work and its truly miraculous discovery. Vermeille found the man's smugness intolerable, and continued to climb the steps leading into the central hall.

Everything was gray — the walls, the carpeting, and the columns — presumably to act as backdrop to the objects being put up for auction. The mahogany counters leading to the main sales room were stacked high with catalogs.

Peter Mansfield, one of Sotheby's vice presidents, was standing near the door to the room. He courteously greeted Adalbert and directed him toward the front row, where a seat had been reserved for him. When he spotted Vermeille, Mansfield seemed slightly embarrassed, as if he wanted to tell him something. But the crowd was beginning to press forward and there was no time. One of his assistants escorted Vermeille to his seat in the third row.

The room held around five hundred, and it was filled. Dozens of people, not finding a free chair, positioned themselves along the sides and at the back. Those without invitations and late arrivers massed outside in the hall in front of television monitors so that they could follow what was happening. Camera crews were setting up equipment in preparation for this historic sale, which was set to begin at 10:15.

The buzz of conversation was nearly deafening. Exclamations and salutations in every language sailed around the room. Facing the center aisle, on a small stage surrounded by long gray curtains, the first painting that was going up for auction was hanging. To its right was a podium. Actually, rather than a podium, it was an ecclesiastical-looking hexagonal pulpit with a canopy. On either side of the pulpit were tables covered in the same gray material, on which sat telephones and computer screens. Elegantly dressed assistants stood ready to take orders from buyers in Tokyo, London,

Geneva, and Paris, or to inquire whether a seller would accept or reject a bid.

Over them all was an enormous screen on which currency conversions would be displayed. The screen was still blank at this point, showing only the words "All Conversions Approximate."

From where he sat, Vermeille had an excellent view. He knew many of the faces present, and nodded his hellos. His eyes landed on Jane Caldwell, whose red hair seemed more flamboyant than ever. Next to her sat Quentin Van Nieuwpoort.

Vermeille was struck at once by the beauty of Jane's profile. He had often thought that profiles were the most revealing angles of vision. Too few realized what they looked like in profile, and made double chins by lowering their head. If they arched their head in the wrong way, a wattle of loose skin dangled from their throats. The little signs of letting go.

He could tell that Jane Caldwell was not among those who let themselves go. She held her head erect, her shoulders back. Her forehead was high and proud. Her magnificent hair was pulled back and up, revealing large temples. An artist would want to draw that head, thought Vermeille. Perhaps not the earlobes. How easily can beauty be marred by so small a feature.

When their eyes met for a second, Vermeille believed he could see a provocative gleam in her green eyes. He couldn't be sure. He forced himself to maintain an expression of complete neutrality, showing no surprise at seeing her here in New York, or seated next to Van Nieuwpoort. Caldwell's financial interest in the Lorrain sale was supposed to be a secret.

At precisely 10:10, the principal auctioneer, a specialist in old masters, entered the room to discreet applause. He walked to the podium like an orchestra conductor, and with slow ceremony took his place on the stand. He gazed out at the crowd for a moment, then picked up the ivory hammer and struck it three times.

The room immediately fell silent. The assistants, like so many acolytes, riveted their gaze on the audience, alert to the slightest movement.

The sale was beginning.

To dignify — and benefit from — the sale of a Claude Lorrain, and to attract buyers of the highest quality and deepest pockets, Sotheby's had planned on selling thirty or so paintings at this auction. Each was a work of considerable value. Some of them were of exceptional quality.

Following well-established tradition, there was a slight delay before the first painting went up for auction. This gave time for the late-arriving VIPs to make their way to their reserved seats.

The work in question was *Virgin and Child Surrounded by Saint Jerome and Saint Sebastian*. It was an altarpiece, painted sometime around 1500 by Pietro Di Domenico of Sienna. That, at least, was the opinion of Sotheby's, as indicated by the asterisk preceding the name. A note at the bottom of the catalog page sent readers to the glossary, where the auction house carefully defined the difference between a work done by the artist — whose name was in large print — and the paintings "attributed" to the painter, either by his "workshop" or "school," or "after the manner of" or "in the style of."

Despite these subtleties, it was a superb work. The

bidding quickly mounted to $118,000, nearly double what had been predicted.

This boded well for the next work, a still life by Versaille's great decorator Jean-Baptiste Monnoyer. The set at the front of the room turned, and as if by magic the Madonna altarpiece disappeared, replaced by a picture of an enormous and overflowing vase of multicolored roses, lilies, and wild flowers.

The painting was projected to go at between $80,000 and $120,000. Bidding started at $60,000. Two or three hands went up. The price leapt quickly by increments of $10,000. When it reached $130,000 only two bidders remained. One, a well-known French dealer, offered $140,000. Her competitor shook his head.

The auctioneer scanned the crowd for a few seconds, and then brought down the hammer. Sold.

That painting disappeared and in its place appeared a work of even greater quality: a view of the port of Recife, painted in 1649 by the Dutch artist Franz Jansz Post, who had accompanied Count Johan Maurits Nassau-Siegen to Brazil. Few documents of this expedition survived and most of Post's works were in museums. The Louvre owned four.

The painting was valued between $300,000 and $500,000. A Dutch collector, determined that Post's painting should stay in its home country, bid the higher amount and got it.

A Brazilian museum, however, got its revenge a few minutes later by offering $684,000 for a panoramic view of the same port of Recife, painted in 1647 by Gillis Peeters, an artist who had gone with Count Naussau-Siegen on his quixotic trip to establish a Dutch realm in northern Brazil.

Sotheby's displayed consummate skill at varying the paintings up for auction, and at stimulating the interest of the buyers.

Some of the works failed to reach their minimum price and were taken out of auction. Others doubled or even tripled their estimated worth. A large portrait of Countess Czernin, painted in 1793 by Élisabeth Vigée-Lebrun during her exile in Vienna, did not reach its estimated worth of $500,000. Neither did two views of Venice's Grand Canal by Bernardo Bellotto.

But Esteban Murillo's portrait of a man in a large black hat, which had been valued between $70,000 and $90,000, went for $270,000.

The auction moved along rapidly, the lots becoming more and more significant. Tension grew. What was of interest was not the esthetic value of the paintings, but the prices they were fetching.

Would a portrait of Madame Boudrey by Jean-Marc Nattier, picturing the young woman as a muse, go for $700,000, as had been predicted? How much would the El Greco that followed it sell for? The painting was a superb crucifixion scene, dating from the end of the sixteenth or early years of the seventeenth century, when the artist was at the height of his powers. In the work, night has fallen on Golgotha, but the luminous skies behind Christ show his triumph over death.

No major El Greco work had gone up for auction in years. A conservative estimate of the painting's value was between $600,000 and $800,000. There was an opening bid of $700,000. Immediately three or four round signs in black plastic, bearing in white the number of a client, went up.

"On my left, seven hundred and fifty thousand dollars. In the middle, eight hundred thousand. In the back, nine hundred thousand dollars."

On the screen, conversion figures whirled, indicating what these amounts meant in francs, marks, and pounds.

When the bidding exceeded $1 million — and showed no sign of slowing — everyone in the room held his breath. Two Japanese buyers and a French dealer, acting on behalf of an unnamed client, were going up against an American, the director of a well-known West Coast museum.

On the phones were German, Swiss, and Italian bidders as well as one from Hong Kong.

At $2 million, only the French dealer and the Chinese bidder remained. With each figure, the assistant on the phone repeated what was bid.

"Will you follow?" she asked.

The French dealer, who was in the room, was beginning to sweat. Finally he threw in the towel. The auctioneer turned to the assistant and instructed her to tell her client that his bid stood. The room went silent.

"Any advance on two million two hundred thousand dollars? Fair Warning."

The expression of Christ on the cross, his eyes turned away in agony and revulsion, might to some have symbolized his horror at being sold to the money lenders in the temple. But nobody attended the irony.

The hammer went down and the spell was broken. The audience burst into applause.

It was now the turn of *The Port of Naples,* by Claude Lorrain.

At most auctions, the lead piece is displayed in the room

from the very beginning, as a way of inspiring bidders. This time was different. The stage turned. A pedestal appeared. The audience gasped.

There was nothing on it.

Immediately it was assumed that Sotheby's was deliberately delaying the appearance of the painting to heighten drama. After all, the works already auctioned off were worth a fraction of this newly discovered Lorrain.

The catalog indicated that the painting was estimated to be worth between $60 and $70 million, but this truly astronomical sum intimidated no one. All the world's museums and all the biggest collectors who did not yet own a Lorrain were going to fight for it with all their resources. The rumor was that *The Port of Naples* might surpass the $75 million hammer price set by van Gogh's *Portrait of Doctor Gachet*.

The tension in the room was palpable. Would the bidding go higher?

After a pause of several minutes, the sales director descended from his pulpit. An older and even more distinguished-looking gentleman took his place. This was Sir John Howard, president and chief executive officer of Sotheby's New York.

Looking formidably dignified in his Savile Row suit, Sir Howard announced in a calm voice that due to reasons entirely beyond Sotheby's control *The Port of Naples* by Claude Gellée, known as Claude Lorrain, would not be put up for sale.

"Ladies and Gentlemen, the auction is at an end," he concluded.

He then climbed down from the podium and left the room.

Absolute silence reigned for nearly ten seconds, after which there was a clearing of throats, a rustling of clothing — and then an explosion of conversation. Journalists ran for the door, people clambered across rows to confer with friends and colleagues. There were loud exclamations of surprise and dismay and disappointment of the sort never before heard in a Sotheby's auction house.

Vermeille focused his gaze on Jane Caldwell, who sat perfectly still. Quentin Van Nieuwpoort got up in a bound, as if stung by a bee, and walked briskly down the aisle.

A quarter of an hour passed. The room emptied out.

Vermeille never took his eyes off Caldwell. She didn't return the look. She looked like a prisoner on whom judgment has been passed.

Leonardo da Vinci used to follow prisoners condemned to death, to watch and record their expressions of suffering and terror. Vermeille continued to stare at Caldwell's face. She was rigid, except her chin. Just perceptibly, it was trembling.

When Van Nieuwpoort returned he whispered something in her ear. She rose to her feet, then sank back slowly into her chair. For the first time, she met Vermeille's gaze, and he could see rage and defiance in her eyes. She was, he had to admit, more beautiful than ever. He forced his expression to remain neutral. For Vermeille, nonetheless, it was a moment of triumph for which he had been waiting for two months.

Should Caldwell have expected something like this of Vermeille? She knew him better than almost anyone. But she had missed his capacity for empathy, without which all other psychological insight is useless. She had perhaps also underestimated his passion for justice, and to what lengths he would go to even the accounts.

154

Vermeille guessed what Van Nieuwpoort was saying to Caldwell. He was telling her that when the painting had been removed from its protective casing the evening before the auction, it had disintegrated. Right in front of all the Sotheby's officials. Within seconds, it had begun to crack and blister, until it had turned entirely to ash.

Vermeille also guessed what happened next. Horrified by the spectacle, Sotheby's officials immediately went into a closed-door meeting. Rather than announce what had happened — particularly since they didn't yet know why it had happened — they decided to proceed with the auction the following day, as planned. They were determined to let the other works up for auction benefit from the enormous publicity given the Lorrain. Were news to leak out it would have had a dampening effect on the spirits of the bidders.

Vermeille kept his gaze on Caldwell's profile, watching its rigidity slowly dissolve. He could only imagine what had gone into making that painting — the research, the materials, the time. Finding some unknown genius to paint it. Making that perfect a copy was nearly a miracle.

She had proven true Jean Cocteau's aphorism, "To make a successful fake is to make the real thing."

Vermeille could imagine her stupefaction, her rage, her confusion, her desperate need to understand what had happened. How could something that had taken so long simply go up in smoke? How had Vermeille succeeded in finding out the identify of his persecutor? What was his part in all this?

With a schadenfreude worthy of his colleague Adalbert, Vermeille imagined Caldwell's feelings. After the rage would come denial, then acceptance. Then agony. That painting had been perfect! Perfect! Vermeille must have known. Vermeille could never have admitted he had authenticated a fake Lorrain. Doing that would have destroyed him. Yet what could he prove? That someone had sent him photographs? Nobody was actually threatened. She needed to talk to someone, yet the only person she could confide in was Van Nieuwpoort. And he was the last person she could confide in.

Quentin Van Nieuwpoort was still talking to her. Vermeille knew he was trying to console her. She was to be congratulated for the picture's having been estimated at the value it was. Sotheby's was willing to seek only restitution for its costs, instead of insisting upon its 20 percent commission, and that would put another fifteen million dollars into their offshore company.

Vermeille imagined this conversation by interpreting Van Nieuwpoort's comforting demeanor and Caldwell's profile. Some color was returning to her cheeks.

That meant she had not yet grasped what was to come. She was still thinking that, yes, the painting was lost but at least they would get the insurance money — enough to live very comfortably for the rest of their lives. She could pay off her debts. The cost of doing the Lorrain copy must have been enormous.

Was she beginning to suspect that he was behind this? Some instinct might have begun to whisper in her ear, but it was only instinct. How could she have guessed that a tweedy French professor of art history would be versed in chemistry — enough at least to concoct and then apply a transparent layer of phosphorus contained within carbon sulfite, such that it would combust in air only after several days of exposure?

Vermeille had spread this invisible film on the back of

the painting before giving it back to the Sotheby's representatives, who then took it to Oxford for packaging. The Lorrain, as per his suggestion, had been immediately put into a case containing an inert gas. By Jane Caldwell.

The painting was a sort of time bomb.

While the work was on tour, Vermeille had trembled at the thought that some accident might set it off before its time. Anything could have gone wrong.

But everything went just right.

Their eyes met again. Her expression revealed confusion — but also dawning realization. That he might be responsible for this disaster was working its way into her consciousness. He saw her expression harden. He thought he could see something dangerous growing in her eyes.

Neither Sotheby's nor the insurers had any reason to suspect Vermeille. Why would they accuse someone who had just verified a painting's authenticity of then destroying it? The notion was preposterous.

Who would they suspect? The last person to have touched the Lorrain before it was sealed in its case. Analysis of the painting's remains by a broker specializing in insuring works of art would doubtless determine the cause of the auto-da-fé. Who, apart from Jane Caldwell, had the knowledge and opportunity to do such a thing? She was famous for her pioneering work in protecting works of art in controlled environments.

And when some anonymous source sent the insurance company an illegal but damning photocopy, providing the names and principals of certain offshore companies, they would learn that Jane Caldwell was also co-owner of the lost masterpiece.

The conclusion would be that she had motive as well as means: she had preferred the insurance money, which was tax-free, to what she might or might not have gotten from the sale of the work at auction — an amount from which Sotheby's would deduct its commission.

The insurers would most likely refuse to pay anything close to the original amount. If they paid any amount at all, it would only be to avoid a trial whose outcome in any case would be disastrous to the reputation of the director of the Oxford Institute for Art Research.

How would Caldwell explain to Quentin Van Nieuwpoort why the insurers were refusing to pay? Would she tell him that not only was their Lorrain a fake, but that Vermeille's certificate had been obtained through extortion?

Vermeille's thoughts drifted away from revenge. He felt more at peace than he had in months. Anger had been his mooring. Now it was setting him loose.

What had happened had changed him. He would be less self-righteous, more humane, less proud, more understanding.

When Caldwell turned her head toward him one last time, Vermeille gave her a look of genuine warmth and recognition — the look that once she had so desperately sought from him.

Then he rose from his chair and walked out of the room. Sunlight was streaming through the windows.